'We were both willed. . .neither give.'

Flicking her a glance that held the derision she had come to loathe, Arden asked, 'Is that the excuse you give yourself?'

'You wouldn't live in England. . .'

'Couldn't live in England. . .and you flatly refused to even consider coming out here to live.'

'And instead of coaxing you stormed off back to the States.'

'You expected me to beg?'

'No.'

'No. You wanted it all, didn't you, Rowan? No compromise.'

'And would you? Have compromised, I mean.'

Emma Richmond was born during the war in north Kent when, she says, 'farms were the norm and motorways non-existent. My childhood was one of warmth and adventure. Amiable and disorganised, I'm married with three daughters, all of whom have fled the nest—probably out of exasperation! The dog stayed, reluctantly. I'm an avid reader, a compulsive writer and a besotted new granny. I love life and my world of dreams, and all I need to make things complete is a housekeeper—like yesterday!'

Recent titles by the same author:

THE BACHELOR CHASE

HAVING IT ALL!

BY
EMMA RICHMOND

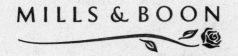

All the characters in this book have no existence outside the imagination of the author, and have no relation whatsoever to anyone bearing the same name or names. They are not even distantly inspired by any individual known or unknown to the author, and all the incidents are pure invention.

*MILLS & BOON and the Rose Device
are trademarks of the publisher.
Harlequin Mills & Boon Limited,
Eton House, 18–24 Paradise Road, Richmond, Surrey TW9 1SR*

© Emma Richmond 1996

ISBN 0 263 79581 0

*Set in 10 on 12 pt Linotron Times
01-9608-50058*

*Typeset in Great Britain by CentraCet, Cambridge
Made and printed in Great Britain*

CHAPTER ONE

'WERE there any calls?'

'A few; I wrote them down. And you're late. You said you'd be half an hour.'

Ignoring her, Arden Harveson strode into his office, grabbed up the little stack of notes and proceeded to read them. Hovering in the doorway, Rowan watched him.

'What does this say?' he demanded, thrusting a piece of paper towards her.

With a little sigh, she walked across to take it from him. 'Outley's gone back to the Keys. . .'

'Outley? Outley? Who the Sam Hill is Outley?'

'Well, I don't know, do I? That's what I was told, and that he's gone back to the Keys!'

'Aughtley!' he corrected her irritably. 'Aughtley!'

'Aughtley, then. Does it matter? You knew who I meant!'

'That's not the point! If you're taking messages, at least make the effort to get them right!'

'Oh, pardon me!' Throwing up a mock salute, she walked away.

'And there's no need for sarcasm! And if that's the only help you're going to be. . .'

'I'm an aromatherapist, Arden, not a secretary!'

'I know what you are.'

'Don't be spiteful; you're the one who asked me to come!'

5

'No, *Hetty* is the one who asked you to come.'

'Then where is she?'

'Coming!' he snapped shortly.

'Then I'll go and wait in her apartment!'

'Do that. Run away, why don't you? It's what you're good at.'

Yes, it was what she was good at. But she couldn't go to his aunt's apartment, no matter how much both he and she might want her to, because it was shut up for the winter. Electricity off, water off.

Her sigh deep, despairing, Rowan leaned against the wall, watching him. This wasn't going to work. It *couldn't* work. Tension was already cramping her muscles, tightening her chest. How in God's name had she ever thought she would cope? Give me a year, she'd pleaded. No, he had said. Now, or not at all. Then go, she'd shouted. And he had.

Fighting for patience, for strength, she made a determined effort not to lose her temper. Just as she'd been fighting ever since she arrived. 'Think pink, Rowan.' Pink was the colour of serenity, or so her long-ago therapist had told her when she'd first embarked on her career. When you feel your temper simmering, think pink. 'Pink,' she repeated as she called the colour into her mind. 'He doesn't mean his insults personally; he's just in a temper. Something or someone has obviously upset him. Count to ten. One, two, three, four, fi—'

'Very funny,' he muttered as he threw himself into the chair behind his desk. 'And what the hell's pink got to do with anything?'

'It keeps me calm.'

'Oh, I've noticed,' he mocked sarcastically.

'Just tell me where she is,' she demanded with desperate patience, 'and if this is some ploy. . .' No, of course it wasn't a ploy; it didn't need his look of derision to tell her that.

'Still in Miami,' he said shortly.

'Then why did she ask me to come? It was urgent, she said.'

'Urgent?' he scoffed with a bitter laugh. 'The only urgency is her damned manipulation.' Leaning back in his chair, his eyes cold, distant, he stated flatly, 'She wanted you to come, my dear Rowan, because she's decided she's dying.'

'Don't be ridiculous! You don't *decide* you're dying! You either are or you aren't.' Pausing, she stared at him worriedly. 'But she is ill, isn't she? When she rang, said I must come urgently, I thought. . .'

'She isn't ill,' he denied brusquely. 'She's a querulous old lady who likes pulling strings. She was supposed to have been here yesterday.'

'Then why isn't she? And why are we going up north? Why couldn't I have gone to see her in Miami?'

'Don't ask.'

'I am asking!'

Tossing his messages onto the desk, he stared at her, his grey eyes hard. Arden always *hated* answering questions. Being *accountable*. Was that why she was persisting? Who knew?

'She wanted to spend Thanksgiving on the Cape.'

'On a *whim*? And I thought that was south of Boston, not north.'

'Arundel. Not Cod.'

'And you allowed it? You shouldn't pander to her,' she muttered disagreeably.

'Do I ever get a choice?'

Abandoning it, not wanting to get into another stupid argument, she sighed. 'She really isn't ill?'

'No. She still has a weak heart, is still supposed to be taking things *easy*, but no, she isn't ill.'

Thanks, Hetty, Rowan thought. Thanks a bunch. She'd rushed out in worry, screwed herself up to meet Arden again, and for what? An old lady's whim. 'So what am I supposed to do in the meantime?' she asked wearily.

'Bait me?' he asked sarcastically.

'I don't bait you. You have to go out again?' she asked with more hope than common sense.

'Maybe. I might need to call in at the office.'

'*Another* office?'

'Yes, *another* office. I have several businesses to run, in case you'd forgotten, so I shall need you to take calls—correctly!'

'Then use your answering machine.'

'Oh, that would be really nice, wouldn't it? I'm sorry I'm not available at present, but please leave a message after the tone and, by the way, I've gone bankrupt!'

'Oh, for goodness' sake!' He'd try the patience of a saint! 'Why don't you have a secretary here?'

'I do; she rang in sick.'

Probably knew what a foul temper he was going to be in, Rowan mused. And how the hell was she supposed to know that he had more than one office? All she did know with any degree of accuracy was how he was as a lover. Mouth tight, she shoved the thought away, refusing to acknowledge that they'd even been *polite* to each other... And what did he mean, bankrupt? He had more businesses than Branson! Fishing fleets, real estate, antiques... They couldn't *all* be failing!

'Are you?' she demanded.

'Am I what?' he asked irritably.

'Going bankrupt?'

'No.'

'Then why say it?'

'Because if left to you I would be! Did Tom ring?'

'Tom who? No,' she replied mutinously in the face of his scowl.

'Then if you've nothing more constructive to say go and look at the hops or something; I'm busy.'

Yes, busy. He'd *always* been busy. As had she. And this continual sniping was destroying her. With a deep sigh, she walked across to the window and stared out at the dismal day. Autumn had been a non-event, or hadn't wanted to play. Whatever the reason, winter—never one to miss an opportunity—had nipped in early and was busily, almost gleefully hurling icy gusts of rain across the harbour. Spiteful, Rowan thought bleakly.

Their reflections in the window were shadowy, distorted, but in no way did they diminish their striking appearances. Her thick mass of hair was the colour of deepest bronze, her creamy skin enhanced rather than marred by the smattering of freckles that would multiply come summer. Her slanted eyes of palest green looked too light, too startling in their setting of dark lashes. There was a hint of passion in the full lower lip of her generous mouth—a promise of warmth.

She looked as though she should have been gracing some tropical isle, a hibiscus in her hair, a sarong to enhance her generous figure, not some tiny office above Boston harbour at the end of October.

And there was Arden, further away from the window, not quite so clearly defined, but defined enough—disturbingly so. And her awareness of him was almost—frightening.

He looked like a rangy wolf. Tall, impressive, the nose aquiline, the mouth firm. Iron-grey hair and eyes to match, and she had never met another man with one tenth of his magnetism—or one tenth of his arrogance. Not a tame man. A man with a hint of danger, violence barely leashed—and it excited her, had always excited her. Instant impact. Living with him had been like living on a knife-edge—and you couldn't live your life trying to balance for ever. At least, she hadn't been able to.

Was this meeting affecting him as much as it was affecting her? She didn't know. His temper, his irritability, might have a different cause. Best never to assume where Arden was concerned. Arden Harveson. Her one-time lover. He lived on one side of the Atlantic and she on the other. Two strong-minded, determined people—and neither would give. And now it was too late even for the choice.

'I could hire a car, drive up. . .' she began.

'You could,' he agreed indifferently.

'Then why don't I?'

'Because I shall be going up there anyway, so it seems a little—pointless, don't you think?' Flicking her a glance, he gave a derisive smile. 'She wants us all to be together.'

For Thanksgiving? she wondered sourly. Hetty hadn't seemed senile the last time they'd talked.

'She's hoping you might distract me from thoughts of my new neighbour,' he prompted her mockingly as he extracted a book from the shelf behind him. Opening it, he picked up his pen and began to write.

'What sort of thoughts?' she asked before she could stop herself.

'Amorous?' he queried hatefully.

'Amor—' Jealousy curled inside her, tightened its grip, and was forcibly dismissed. He had not sounded lover-like. And she no longer wanted him. Don't lie, Rowan; don't lie. She thought that she would *always* want him. And that was the most depressing thought of all. 'And are they?'

'Perhaps.'

'And Hetty doesn't like it?'

'No.'

Remembering Arden's earlier words, remembering the long, rambling telephone conversation with her godmother, she queried disbelievingly, 'And so she's decided to die? Out of spite?'

'Not exactly,' he denied, with a little smile that wasn't even remotely amused. 'She's decided that now might be a good time to re-ignite your interest in me. Hence the urgent invitation.'

'And yours in me? But we don't have any interest in each other, do we?'

'No.'

No. So now you know, Rowan. 'And so, in effect, having informed me of her twisted reasoning, you're telling me what? Not to take any notice of what she says?'

'*I'm* not telling you anything,' he asserted. 'Merely

explaining her thoughts on the subject—and warning you of her approaching death.'

'Which she isn't really approaching, only pretending to, because she doesn't like your liaison with the next-door neighbour. Is that right?'

'Perfectly.'

'Emotional blackmail.'

'Of course it is. But not mine. I'm merely the fool caught in the middle.'

'You've never been *mere* in your life.' Or a fool, she added silently. 'And what, pray, does she expect me to do about it?'

'Lure me away?'

With a scoffing laugh, she jeered, 'Very likely.'

'Bitter, Rowan?'

'No.' Not bitter, just—disillusioned. And aching.

Looking up, pen poised, he drawled, 'You're clever, attractive, amusing, independent, confident, opinionated. . .'

'Just like you.'

'Yes, just like me—and we differ on every conceivable subject, don't we? If I say black, you'll say white. . .'

'Not deliberately. Not just for the sake of it.'

'No?'

'No.'

The phone rang, and, punctiliously polite, he murmured, 'Excuse me,' and picked it up.

Turning back to the view, she stared without interest at the ships, or boats, or whatever they were in the harbour. Heavy rain pitted the surface of the water, made everything look grey. And she shouldn't have come. She had *known* that.

'She's at Logan,' he said abruptly.

'Logan?'

'The airport.'

'Oh.'

Capping his pen, slamming the book shut, he stood, hooked his leather jacket off the back of the chair and put it on. 'Are you staying here?'

'No, I'll come with you.'

He gave an indifferent nod and picked up his keys, then her case, and waited.

'I didn't know she was coming into the airport. I could have waited there, couldn't I?'

'Yes.'

Mouth tight, she preceded him out and across to the lift. Elevator, she reminded herself. Americans called them elevators.

Emerging into the street, coat collar turned up against the rain, she bumped into someone, turned, smiled, apologised—and he did a double take, grinned, turned to walk backwards along the street, grin still in place.

An edge to his voice, Arden derided her, 'Still knocking 'em dead, I see.'

'Of course.' The game had to be played, didn't it?

With a twisted smile, he locked the front door and urged her along to his car. Slinging her case in the boot, he continued his baiting. 'Poor devil. Am I likely to get a knife in my back for even talking to you?'

'Don't be stupid.'

'Oh, I'm never stupid, Rowan. Never.'

Yes, you are, she wanted to argue. Once, you were very stupid. But she wouldn't, because he didn't think that he had been. He thought that he'd been lucky.

With automatic courtesy he held the passenger door
open for her. 'I wonder if you'll still be driving the
male population wild when you're an old lady?' he
asked idly. 'What are you now? Twenty-six?'

'You know how old I am. Twenty-seven.'

'Just.'

'Just,' she agreed with a little inclination of her head.
And she did not drive men wild. Only disturbed them
a bit.

And when he'd climbed in beside her she made the
mistake of looking into his eyes, and her stupid heart
turned over, because, whatever she might tell herself,
whatever she might pretend, he still had the power to
stir her blood, excite her, and he was, without excep-
tion, the most masculine, the most vitally attractive
man she had ever met.

'How was the course?' he asked mockingly. Temper
had obviously been abandoned.

'What?'

'You've been on a course, haven't you? In France?'

'Oh, yes.' Aware of him in a way she didn't want to
be aware—of every breath, every muscle—she fought
to pull herself together. 'Hetty told you?'

'Hetty? No. Hetty and I very rarely discuss you.'

How dismissive. How utterly and totally dismissive.
'And is that supposed to make me feel diminished?'
she asked with a twisted smile.

'Not at all. A mere statement of fact. *Does* it make
you feel diminished?'

'No.' And it didn't; just—miserable. But this time
emotion must not get in the way, and so it must not
matter how he knew where she'd been; she should just
pretend that he'd asked nicely, as though he was

actually interested. 'Yes,' she repeated, and if her jaw was a little bit gritted perhaps he wouldn't notice. And is the moon made of cheese, Rowan? she asked herself.

'Interesting, was it?'

'Yes,' she agreed. 'Informative. I'm glad I went.' Banal, but better than sniping, better than overreacting to his blatant provocation. Better than falling apart at the seams because he could so easily disorder her senses. . . Senses she did not *want* disordered, and so different tactics must be used.

Aloofness wouldn't work because he had already made her lose her composure, and so she would follow his lead—scoff, turn his own derision against him. And if he thought her hard, uncaring, so be it. She would not live her life on his opinion of her. But she damned Hetty for her interfering. Damned herself for allowing it.

Turning her head, trying for a bit of apparent interest, she stared through the window, watched the awnings on the shops they passed, watched them billow and strain at their supports then droop limply as the wind briefly died. Forcing herself to remain calm, she tried to ignore Arden's disruptive presence, the tension he could still so easily generate in her.

'Not many tourists about,' he commented with that hateful jeering inflexion that always made her want to hit him.

'No. Maybe the rain frightened them away. Oh, this is absurd!' she exclaimed. 'We're both adult; surely we can think of something to talk about other than the weather?'

His smile was feral, and she began to feel goaded,

out of control. 'You erupt into my life like a genie
from a bottle—'

'I thought you erupted into mine,' he argued
smoothly, 'although hopefully the transport was a little
more conventional.'

'And actually being *nice*!' she mocked.

'Polite at any rate.'

'Why wouldn't you be? You had a lucky escape.
You said so.'

'So I did.'

Turning away, defeated, she asked what she had
been intending *not* to ask. 'How *did* you know I'd been
in France?' Because he'd rung her club, she suddenly
realised. That was the only way he *could* have known.
'I hope you didn't upset my staff.'

'Now why would I do that?' he drawled in lazy
amusement.

'Because you stir up trouble just for the hell of it.
Or you used to,' she observed moodily. 'And, if Hetty
didn't tell you, in order to know that I'd been in France
you would, presumably, have had to make enquiries at
my club. Unless, of course, you're psychic.'

'Mmm, unless that, of course.'

'Arden,' she warned as she teetered on the edge of
temper, 'just answer the question.'

His amusement still very much in evidence—or,
rather, she thought, his pretend amusement, because
she couldn't for the life of her imagine why he might
be amused—he agreed, 'Yes, I enquired, and no, I did
not upset them. Satisfied?'

'Marginally, which brings us back to why you were
asking. You've never rung before. Have you?' she
asked worriedly.

'No.'

'Then why now?'

'Because I thought you might like warning that Hetty was intending for us all to be together.'

'Oh.'

'But you weren't there, you were in France; and because I thought you might not want your—"staff",' he parodied her, 'to know your business I did not, therefore, leave a message.'

'Oh.'

Reaching the airport, he parked—illegally, she was sure—in the cab rank. 'Wait here,' he ordered offhandedly. 'I'll go and find her.' Jamming his hands into his pockets, he strode off. More than one person turned to watch him. And not only women.

With a deep sigh, she leaned back into the upholstery and stared at the airport—an airport she had left only a few hours earlier. Tiredness was beginning to catch up with her, exhaustion to nibble at the edges of her spirit. Barely back from France, she'd had a shower, change of clothes, exchanged one set of luggage for another, and been off again. To this.

The door was wrenched open and she jumped. Stared at an angry Arden. No, not angry—disgusted.

Glancing behind him, seeing no sign of her godmother, she asked weakly, 'Where is she?'

Face set, he didn't answer but merely climbed in, fired the engine and drove out of the airport as though the devil were behind him.

'Arden! Where's Hetty?'

'Quincy Market,' he drawled flatly. 'She wanted to do some shopping.'

'Quincy Market?' she echoed faintly. 'Where's that?'

'Boston.'

'But why?'

'Why?' he queried. 'Well, now, there could be any number of reasons,' he mused sarcastically. 'Thoughtlessness? A desire to punish me for wrongs only she perceives? A—'

'But she knew you were picking her up! She rang and asked you to!'

'Of course she did; that's why she left a message at the desk. And if, when I finally catch up with her, I take her to task on how she expects me to run my business, entertain an ex-mistress *and* run backwards and forwards to the airport she will look astonished and enquire if I'm feeling tired.'

Oh, God.

With enough sense—just—to know that it would be best not to answer, she watched the traffic. The remainder of the return trip was accomplished in silence.

What a way to see Boston, she thought gloomily.

He parked, sighed, ordered tersely, 'You go that way, I'll go this. And don't be long; I'm illegally parked.' Striding off, hands jammed once more into his jacket pockets, he disappeared into the cobbled market.

A few stallholders selling sweatshirts were braving the awful weather and watched Arden stride off, and they grinned at her. Probably thought they'd had a tiff. Hah. They should have seen the 'tiff' they'd had last summer. Now *that* had been worth watching!

'Faneuil Hall' was written over the arch, and she frowned. 'Quincy Market?' she asked the nearest stallholder, and he pointed.

'Oh, thank you.'

'Love the accent, ma'am.' He grinned and she gave a reluctant laugh. 'Have a nice day.'

With a wry smile, she exclaimed, 'It certainly couldn't get any worse!' Don't tempt fate, she warned herself belatedly. With Arden and Hetty, worse could turn so easily into catastrophe.

Nearly ricking her ankle on the rain-slicked cobbles, her hair getting wetter by the minute, she hurried towards the long building on her left, but the little exchange had cheered her, calmed her. However momentarily.

Easing her way through the crowded food hall, senses assaulted by the many smells wafting at her, not to mention the wetness of everybody, the revolting smell of damp wool, the hazards to her shins from dripping umbrellas held point downwards, she peered into every nook and cranny, getting some very funny looks in the process.

Making her way to the opposite side, she squeezed past stallholders selling everything from corn dollies to wax candles, investigated every cellar, and got not one glimpse of her godmother.

Did he mean her to look in the other building as well? She supposed so. Pushing outside, thankful for some fresh air, she turned up her coat collar against the rain and walked across to look in all the shops opposite—shops it would have been nice to linger in, shops that sold things she pathetically yearned for.

Upstairs, downstairs, attacked on all sides by bulky carrier-bag-wielding shoppers, she finally made her way back to the car—and a waiting Arden.

'Nothing?' she asked worriedly.

'No.'

'Now what?'

'We'll try her apartment, and if she's not there we'll go back to my office, see if she's left a message. *Another* one. She might even be there in *person*.'

'It's not my fault,' she said quietly.

'I didn't say it was. Get in the car.'

Rowan got in the car.

Pushing her dripping hair off her face, staring out at the wet streets in the hope of spotting a determined elderly lady, she sighed. Oh, Hetty, what on earth are you playing at? she thought. She must *know* that Arden wasn't the most patient of people. And she certainly knew that Rowan wasn't!

Rowan needed order in her life—and Hetty wasn't one to be ordered. Neither was Arden. She had *known* that, but out of temper or ignorance or just plain stupidity she had still tried.

There had been three months of passion—and a continuing knowledge that it had to end. Compromise hadn't been in either of their vocabularies, and two people couldn't conduct a love affair thousands of miles apart. She had been attracted to him, affected by him, but she hadn't known if it was love. Her body had wanted his, her heart had misbehaved when he was near, but her mind had continued to weigh the odds. Surely, if you love, heart and mind were one?

Yet the face she showed the world, the face that Arden saw, wasn't necessarily the face of truth. As a child, it had been the face of insecurity and a determination to prove herself. At twenty-seven it was the face of success and confidence—and a determination to live her life as *she* wanted.

'You think she'll be there?' she asked quietly.

'I would know?'

'There's no need to be sarcastic.'

'True.'

With a sigh she stared through the window, tried to see *something* of the city. 'Is that the State House?'

He flicked a glance to his left. 'Yes. Beacon Hill,' he added a few moments later. 'Acorn Street.' He slowed so that she could view the little cobbled hill, its houses and lamps so very reminiscent of England, and she supposed that she should be grateful for the small consideration.

'Charles Street,' he muttered, and again she dutifully looked. 'Brick sidewalks, gas-lit streetlamps. One of the most charming areas in the city.'

'It's nice,' she said inadequately.

'Yes.' Swerving round a yellow cab, he pulled up at the kerb.

'Is this where Hetty lives?'

'Yes.' He climbed out, slammed his door and walked inside.

With an exasperated grunt, she followed him into the foyer where an elderly man sat behind an ornate desk. The porter, she supposed.

He smiled at Arden, and then his smile widened when he caught sight of Rowan—as most men's smiles widened when they caught sight of Rowan. Wet and bedraggled as she was, she was still beautiful.

'Another moth to the flame,' Arden said in a disparaging aside. 'Has my aunt been by?' he asked the man.

'No, sir.' He looked worried, puzzled. 'Were you expecting her to be here?'

'No,' Arden denied disgustedly. 'Today I don't expect anything. Thanks.' Taking Rowan's arm, he urged her towards the exit, and the porter grabbed an umbrella and escorted them.

'I told you to wait in the car.'

'No, you didn't.'

'I implied it.'

Biting down hard on another angry, pointless retort, she sighed. Just go with the flow, she told herself. Just go with the flow.

Hungry because she'd had no lunch, tired because she'd had no sleep on the plane and very little on the ferry from France, she stumbled, and Arden gave her a look of dislike. Did he think that she'd done it deliberately? Probably. One more effort, she urged herself. And the worst was over, wasn't it? She'd met him again. And survived.

Catching sight of herself in the mirrored panel by the front entrance, she grimaced. In repose she had a haughty face. The face of a siren. And then she grinned, because no siren she'd ever heard of had a tangled mop of ginger hair.

That hair brought the real Rowan to life—the Rowan she constantly tried to suppress because otherwise no one took her seriously. And so the girl with the wicked sense of fun, the caring, delightful companion that Arden had sometimes glimpsed but had never been quite sure of because that side of her had been overlaid by rigid determination, had been hidden away inside. And he had never understood that her behaviour had been caused by fear—fear of losing her independence, her security. And so she had lost him. Made a conscious, deliberate decision to part.

'Practising?' he asked derisively.

'Of course. Don't want to get stale, do I?' It was

maddening how those flip answers always seemed to be there, waiting in the wings, so to speak, despite her determination to be different. Another form of hiding.

'And if she's not at your office?' she asked tiredly. 'What then?'

'We drive up the coast. You can cope with that, can't you, Rowan? Another few hours in my company?'

'I can, yes. Can you?' she asked sweetly.

'Of course.'

Of course. His strength of mind was even greater than hers. 'You really think she'll be able to make her way up there?'

'Why not? She managed to get herself from Miami, didn't she? And such a pity to spoil her little game, and the doctor did say she wasn't to be upset unnecessarily.'

'You're the one who's upsetting her.'

'No, I'm the one who's causing her to scheme,' he corrected her. 'You not going is what would upset her.'

'But I am going.'

'Oh, goody.'

And it was all so familiar, this sharpening of swords, back-and-forth fencing. And she must stop it, because it could erupt into—something else. As it so often had.

Aware that the porter was hovering, umbrella raised, she smiled, moved towards the door. They were escorted out to the car and the wretched man even bowed, which instead of amusing her, as it would normally have done, irritated the hell out of her.

'Ma'am?' He opened the door, waited, and Rowan climbed in. It was gently closed. He then escorted Arden round to his door, keeping him safely dry.

'Obsequious, wasn't he?' she said waspishly as Arden fired the engine.

'You mean he isn't like that to everyone?'

'Oh, shut up; stop trying to make me laugh.'

'No, that would be heinous, wouldn't it? Put your insecurities away, Rowan, and do up your seat belt.'

'I don't have any insecurities,' she said. Now. Now that he was no longer in her life to generate them. And she wished, not for the first time, that there was no need to keep hiding her feelings—not just from Arden but from everyone.

She sometimes felt as though she was on an express train to nowhere. Years of striving, fighting to be her own person, years of success and reward, and for what? No one ever acknowledged her success, or praised it. And was that really why she had done all that she'd done? For acclaim? Not a very laudable ambition.

And what did Arden think about her, really feel about her? Not that she would ever ask, but it did seem rather absurd that everything she had done, achieved this last year had been partly due to him. And she'd done it to show him, like a child shouting in the dark. To prove that she had been right and he wrong.

Only, of course, it wasn't as simple as that. Life never was. Financial and business rewards brought their own satisfaction, but would they ever make up for what was lost? And had she chosen differently would she now be wondering about that other choice? Afraid of losing her individuality, her identity, she had ended up alienating a man most women would die for.

With a troubled sigh, knowing that it was partly

exhaustion that was prompting these troublesome thoughts, she fitted her seat belt into its slot.

The sensible course, the intelligent course would be to ignore Hetty's machinations and Arden's inexplicable desire to be helpful and return to London. To security, to her health club, where she was mistress of her own fate. Yet where Arden was concerned was she ever sensible? And she loved Hetty—and if she was dying... No, hard to imagine that strong spirit quenched—but if Hetty did die and she had returned to London without seeing her she would never forgive herself, would always have it on her conscience.

But was Arden telling the truth? He didn't always. He bent the rules to suit himself. Yet what possible reason could he have for telling her about Hetty's schemes? And now they were going north. Perhaps his new neighbour was going too. Perhaps they could all be chums together. Compare notes, she mused a trifle bitterly. Was she pretty, this neighbour of his? Biddable?

Her cheek against the side-window, she stared out at the rain-lashed town. 'Is that Boston Common?'

'Mmm, set aside to quarter British troops at the start of the Revolutionary War. Trying to establish links with England, Rowan?'

'Maybe.'

'Washington Street,' he commented. 'Filene's Basement for bargains.'

'If I come back,' she pointed out.

'If you come back.' And as they drove he continued to point things out. 'Downtown Crossing, Faneuil Hall where we were earlier.'

And it was all very well having these places pointed

out, she thought crossly, but it didn't give her a chance to go and *see* them, did it?

'Paul Revere House,' he continued laconically. 'You know about Paul Revere?'

'Yes,' she muttered.

'Old North Church. All part of the Freedom Trail.' Halting briefly, he pointed across the rain-soaked harbour. 'U.S.S. Constitution, Old Ironsides, and, further off, see that tall monument? Bunker Hill, where the famous battle took place.'

She gave a dispirited nod.

Turning the car, he drove back the way they'd come until they reached the other end of the harbour. 'Boston Tea Party Ship. And if you're lucky you might see them toss a case of tea over the side. Not real tea, of course. Not this time.'

'Don't patronise me, Arden.'

'Sorry,' he apologised insincerely. Halting once more at his office, they both saw the square of paper pinned to the door. He climbed out and wrenched it free.

'She's gone on ahead,' he explained frustratedly as he returned to the car. 'Got tired of waiting. And if she wants to die,' he added darkly as he pulled back into the traffic, 'she is surely lining up several ways to get her wish.'

'And leaving us a nice little unchaperoned drive up to Maine. Well, that will be cosy. Or was that the plan all along?' she added stupidly, goading him just that little bit too far.

The words barely out of her mouth, he slammed the car to a halt, leaned across and fitted his hand round her neck.

CHAPTER TWO

'DON'T,' Arden said through his teeth.

'I was only—'

'I *know* what you were only! Do you *really* think I want a red-headed little witch disrupting my life again? Well, *do* you? You balance me on the edge, Rowan,' he warned savagely. 'You surely do do that.'

'I—'

'Just get it through your head! I no longer want you! I have a need in my life for some peace and tranquillity, not to be constantly disrupted by temper and aggravation!'

'You think *I* don't?'

'I have *no* idea!'

'Well, *I* do!' Slapping his hand away, she stormed, 'You think *I* find this easy? *I* didn't ask to come! *I* didn't ask for you to react to me like a—like a. . .'

'Yes?' he asked softly, and his face was close again, his mouth a scant fraction from hers, and if she leaned forward just the tiniest bit her mouth would brush his, his breath would mingle with hers. Barely aware what they were arguing about, she watched the movement of his lips and desire negated thought, cramped her lungs.

'You think my foul mood is because of you?' he continued, unaware, unmoved. 'And you call *me* arrogant!'

'What?' Snapping her eyes up to his with a jerky

little movement, she leaned away, and to her relief he returned to his own side of the car.

'I did not want you here,' he continued more moderately but still with that air of suppressed violence. 'Hetty did. I did not even know until two days ago that she'd invited you.'

Shocked, eyes still wide, breathing uneven, Rowan took a a moment to react. 'Then why did you ring my club?' she whispered. 'You said—'

'I lied. It was overreaction. Anger at Hetty's interference. I rang to tell you not to come.'

'Then why didn't you ring later?' She frowned. 'Leave a message?'

He gave a mirthless smile. 'Because when I considered it rationally I decided I no longer cared.' Knocking the car into gear, he drove on.

Shaken, she drew in a ragged breath. But he'd thought that he cared? Until he'd considered it rationally. Which meant. . .

'I need to go across to Cambridge, call in at the house for a few minutes.'

Unable to find her voice, she nodded.

'I'll make a detour round Harvard. It's worth seeing.'

'Thank you.'

'Don't sulk. You ask for all you get.'

'And that's supposed to comfort me?' she asked bitterly.

His laugh was abrupt, unamused. 'It's been a foul week,' he added, but whether in explanation or apology she didn't know. Nor did she intend to ask.

'Harvard Square,' he explained quietly. 'The centre of Cambridge activity since the seventeenth century.'

She'd read about it, heard about it, and the reality

was very, very different from her imaginings. It was
beautiful, but she wasn't, now, in the mood for
sightseeing.

She dutifully looked while her mind continued to
play back his earlier, savage words. The buildings could
have been transported from England—such clean
lines, such—warmth. They felt familiar and special—
and yet so different.

'Were you here?' she asked stiltedly.

'Yes.'

'It's very nice.'

He gave her a mocking smile. 'How to damn with
faint praise?'

'What did you expect?'

'Honesty?'

'I am being honest. It *is* nice, but, unlike you, I find
it very hard to switch from one mood to another in
forty seconds.'

'Practice.'

Savagely sweet, she queried, 'Advice or boasting?'
And he laughed, shook his head.

'You should have been smacked as a child.'

Yes, she thought sadly, smacking might have been
kinder than the emotional blackmail she'd received.
And, staring out at the narrow streets, she felt a wave
of unbelievable poignancy, because she could have
walked here, perhaps known some of these people
who meandered along these narrow streets, maybe
browsed in that bookshop, worn one of the sweatshirts,
the name emblazoned across the front.

'Winthrop Square, also seventeenth century,' he
continued. 'Now a public park. Not to be compared, of

course, to your own ancient piles. Our history being—
newer.'

She didn't know if he was being ironic.

'And here we are.'

'Here we are where?'

'My home.'

Staring round her in astonishment—at mansions, for
goodness' sake—she glanced at him to see if he was
joking. He obviously wasn't. 'You live *here*?'

'Yes. Loyalist mansions at the time of the
Revolution. I won't be long.' He climbed out, pushed
open a high wrought-iron gate and disappeared along
a tree-lined path.

He lived *here*? she thought with a hollow laugh. This
was where she could have lived? He had really
expected that she would come *here*? Start up her own
little business? Practise *aromatherapy*? And, if she had
known that this was where, how he lived, her refusal
would have been even more vehement than it had
been.

'I will not live in America,' she had said. No discussion, no leeway, just a flat refusal, because she had not
known America. Her judgement had been based on
books, films—and that was no sort of knowledge at all.

She had never wanted to come to the States. She
didn't know why. Perhaps because it had been hard
enough to cope in England. But the reality, this reality,
was so very far from her imaginings. And the people
she had so far met had all been nice, friendly, polite. . .
And why wouldn't they be? People were people wherever you went.

But had she known that it *was* like this would she
have come? She didn't know. The timing had been so

impossibly wrong, Arden so impossible to live with. He'd exasperated her, invigorated her, made her feel violent and unsettled. There hadn't seemed an answer to the dilemma of what to do, so where had been the point of even asking the question? Unless she'd capitulated, and she hadn't been able to do that.

She had known that he was wealthy, but not as wealthy as he must be if he could afford to live here. In a *mansion*, for goodness' sake! And she really didn't know whether she could have coped with that.

Better not to think, she reminded herself, and fortunately, true to his word, he was back in a few minutes, carrying a small grip. Tossing it into the back of the car, he climbed in, then hesitated, key in the ignition.

'You want me to apologise?' he asked quietly.

'No.'

He gave an odd smile, but it *was* a smile. 'You do goad me sometimes, Rowan. You always did.'

Yes. Whether it be into passion or anger. They did it to each other. One spark short of a conflagration— because both had always drawn back at the last minute, retaining, however tenuously, a semblance of control. 'We had some almighty rows, didn't we?' she mused quietly.

'Yes.'

'Do you think it would ever have worked? *Could* ever have worked?' Her voice sounded wistful and she hadn't meant it to. Hadn't wanted it to. 'If we'd both lived in the same country?'

'Who knows?' Twisting the key, he started the engine, turned the car around and drove off towards the major route that would take them up north. New Hampshire, Vermont, Maine. Names to conjure with, places she had read about, heard about and was now going to visit—with the man she would have visited them with had the choice been easy. And if it had been easy they would have gone as lovers, not as—strangers.

'Was this really Hetty's idea?' she asked quietly.

'Of course. You think it was mine?'

'No. You've already said. . . I mean. . .' She didn't know what she meant but it certainly wasn't that he so desperately wanted her company that he had engineered this trip. Biting her lip, she returned her attention to the wet scenery. 'I only meant that it seemed—incomprehensible.'

'It is incomprehensible—to us. But not to Hetty, and looking for reasons—*any* reasons—where she is concerned is an exercise in futility.'

'Then it isn't because of your neighbour?'

'Patricia? No, Patricia was a convenient peg to hang it on. She wants us back together. You *know* that.'

'Yes.' Every time they met it was Hetty's constant litany. But Rowan didn't know why.

'And why make such an issue out of everything?'

'I don't. Just. . .'

'Just don't like being wrong, do you? That's what sticks in your throat.'

'It isn't,' she insisted. Was that what he really thought? That she was a spoilt little madam who always found suspicions where none existed? Well, certainly he thought that she was spoilt. But then people always thought only children were spoilt—and that was the biggest joke of the century.

If things had come easy, she would have come to America with him. Maybe would have come, she mentally qualified; only where was the point in defending herself? At the end of the day what difference did it make? But why was it that of all the people she had ever loved, who had ever professed to love her, not one had ever seemed to see her as she really was?

All her life she'd had to fight for every inch of space, suppress her true nature in order to survive, be the person she needed to be. And that was what prompted the temper, the outbursts: fighting to make people believe she was capable, not an empty-headed fool. Why did no one see that? Not Arden, her father, her mother, nor Hetty.

And then she wondered, perhaps for the first time, what her behaviour *might* have done to him. If he'd loved her. He was a proud man, and having the girl he'd professed to love refuse even to contemplate uprooting herself and going to live in another country must have dented that pride considerably. Had he been hurt? As she had been? Or was he just bitter and disillusioned? Funny, but she'd always only ever considered it in her own terms, how it had affected her, blamed him for his intransigence.

The long silence was building tension, making her jumpy—not that it seemed to be affecting him, she decided moodily. Not now. But as she continued to watch him, take in those oh, so familiar features, it began to feel as though time had never passed. That it was then, not now.

They halted briefly at the toll-booth. Giving herself a desperate mental shake, she quickly averted her eyes from his strong profile, from the smile he gave the girl taking his money, but it didn't stop the thoughts, the memories—memories she had never allowed herself until now.

Focusing again on his face, she cast about in her mind for an innocuous subject. 'Is there snow up there yet? In the north?'

He shook his head.

'But there is sometimes by now, isn't there?'

'Mmm, sometimes,' he agreed.

He sounded cool again, remote, and wouldn't it be funny if he too was pretending? Pie in the sky, Rowan, she told herself; he isn't pretending, and no amount of wishing will ever make it different.

Not that she wished it different, she assured herself, but it might have been nice to be friends. And if he hadn't always insisted that he knew what was best for her. . .issued an ultimatum. . . Always the wrong thing to do with Rowan. And now he was back in her life, however temporarily, and she had to cope with that.

'Now what are you thinking?' he demanded with only light mockery. 'So many weighty matters to ponder, Rowan?'

For a moment she was tempted to give an offhand answer and then decided to be honest. 'I was wondering if your indifference was real.'

'Toward you, do you mean?'

'Mmm.'

Taking his time, obviously needing to think about it, or careful not to say something he might later regret, he admitted slowly, 'I'm not indifferent about what happens to you, not indifferent to your fate. Just indifferent to what happened between us. Although maybe that's an oversimplification. I can remember the good times we had with a certain amount of pleasure.'

Her sigh was soft, reflective. 'Yes, and there were some good times, weren't there?'

'Yes.'

'But we were both too strong-willed, both too arrogant, weren't we? Neither of us would give.'

Flicking her a glance that held the derision she had come to loathe, he asked, 'Is that the excuse you give yourself?'

'It's not an excuse. You wouldn't live in England...'

'Couldn't live in England. My work was here, my responsibilities, and you flatly refused to even consider coming out here to live.'

'And instead of coaxing, soothing my fears, allowing me time to get used to the idea you stormed off back to the States.'

'You expected me to beg?'

'No.'

'And if I had given you time, would you have agreed?' he asked with that blandness she so hated.

'I don't know.' A lie. Because she didn't think she would have. She'd had a plan—a plan that had kept her sane for too many years for it to be abandoned for love. And perhaps she was only now coming to realise how—sad that was.

'No. You wanted it all, didn't you, Rowan? No compromise.'

'And would you? Have compromised, I mean.'

'I did compromise, for as long as I was able. *I* was the one who flew back and forth. *I* was the one who gave.'

Until he could give no more.

Theirs had been a chance meeting, because in all the years of her knowing that Hetty had a nephew she had never met him until last year. Hetty had always visited her in England—*still* always visited her in England. Until now.

Hetty's father had been a diplomat, stationed in London, and Hetty and Rowan's grandmother had gone to school together. Best friends. And when Hetty had returned to the States they had kept in touch, visited, and she had come over to be Rowan's godmother.

But Rowan had never met Arden until he had come over last year to buy up the antiques that he exported to the States and had called in to drop off some things from Hetty. . . Instant attraction, chemistry, call it what you will, but it had accelerated into passion. And it had never occurred to her, then, that there would not be a happy ending. That there would have to be a choice. Between her plan and his love.

Eight years older than herself, he'd been a man, not a boy, and he had excited her—still excited her—had intimidated her a little too, if she was honest. He didn't intimidate her now, perhaps because she was older, wiser. A natural progression. Now she could hold her own in an argument intelligently.

Oh, yes? You've been behaving really intelligently since you arrived, have you? she asked herself derisively. With a sad little smile she mentally qualified that she would be able to hold her own *if* they ever managed to finish a conversation! Had they ever argued rationally? Or was that, too, one of the factors that had led to the ultimate breakdown of their stormy relationship?

And why? Why had they never been able to talk properly, all cards on the table? Because he always thought he knew the answers and never wanted explanations? Or was it that she had never wanted him to know of her upbringing? Had never wanted to let him see what her parents had *really* been like to make her the way she was? An undeserved loyalty. On the one hand, all of them had treated her like a woman, and, on the other, like a child who didn't know her own mind.

Stifling a yawn, she allowed her mind to drift, and when he stopped and climbed out to fill up with petrol—gasoline, she reminded herself with a tiny smile—she watched him. He looked competent, exciting, important. *Was* competent, exciting... And it could all have been so different.

She watched him walk inside to pay, and as he emerged a little girl skipped out beneath his arm and would have run straight into the path of a slowly moving car if Arden's reactions hadn't been so excellent. He scooped her up, twisted her into his arms, said something, and she gave him a gap-toothed grin and wound her arms round his neck. He laughed and returned her to her frightened mother.

And wasn't it odd how children automatically trusted him? Rowan mused. So why hadn't she? Because she'd no longer been a child?

Sliding behind the wheel, tossing the receipt onto the dashboard, he chuckled, 'I think she liked me.'

'Of course she did,' Rowan commented drily. 'She's female.'

He gave her a thoughtful look and she bit her lip and shrugged. Why pretend? He *was* attractive to members of the opposite sex, whether they be six or sixty. She'd never denied that.

'Tired?' he asked as he pulled smoothly away.

'A bit,' she admitted.

'Mmm, talking can have that effect—and it's been such a stressful day, hasn't it?' he added with teasing humour.

Fighting her own smile, because *this* was the Arden so hard to resist, she nodded.

'And there's really no shame in allowing yourself to be driven, even if it is by your hated ex-lover.'

'I don't hate you,' she protested.

'No?' he asked with rather mocking disbelief. 'Just the space I take up? The way I tread all over your independence? Hate that, don t you, Rowan? And not only *from* me.'

'Yes, she hated it. But had he never wondered why? And he spoke as though everything that had happened had been entirely her own fault, because of her determination. And although that was partly true it wasn't the whole reason. More a case of cause and effect.

'Stop frowning,' he reproved. 'You'll get lines.'

'Hm? Oh, sorry,' she apologised absently without changing her expression. '*Is* that the impression I give?' she asked him. 'That I'm fiercely independent?'

'Mmm-hmm. Aren't you?' he asked mockingly.

'Not fiercely!'

'No?'

'No.'

'Yet you insisted, with great vehemence as I remember, that that was the reason you wouldn't come to the States.'

'Not the only reason,' she said quietly. 'It was a big step. It frightened me. I wouldn't have known anyone... And if no one would take me seriously in

England, what hope did I have that they would here? And to have married you without really knowing you at all... Well, even you had to see that it would have been stupid.'

'I did see that. I expected you would stay with Hetty until you were sure.'

Yes, and then he would have done the same as her father—kept her safe, not allowed her to take risks, or at least pooh-poohed them. A gentle imprisonment, admittedly, but so unutterably frustrating. She'd needed to learn, grow, *be* someone. 'I'd begun to believe in myself, Arden, discovered that I could do things. That I had a brain, a good business sense, that I was actually a person I quite liked. And I knew that I needed the chance to prove myself.'

'Which you could have done in the States.'

'Not in Cambridge, I couldn't,' she said drily. 'Even *you* have to see that!'

'The people in Cambridge are no different to people anywhere else.'

'They looked as though they were—No,' she corrected herself, 'their *houses* did.'

'Then you could have set up your little business empire in Boston, Somerville, Chelsea.'

'But I didn't *know* that. *Now* I do, but not then.'

'And now is too late,' he agreed mockingly, as though she had implied likewise.

'Yes. Now is too late.' And he hadn't *really* wanted a working wife. He'd wanted someone tame, someone to show off, preside over his dinner parties—not a 'red-headed little witch' who wanted to build her own empire.

'And to emphasise your independence,' he con-

tinued, 'to underline that you'd never had any intention of our relationship becoming permanent, you
proudly showed me the establishment you were going
to rent and hung onto the arm of a besotted young
man.'

'Yes, much to his astonishment,' she finally admitted. 'He'd come in to give an estimate for shelving. I'd
never seen him before in my life.'

Staring at her, bitter realisation in his eyes, he gave
a rather self-mocking laugh.

'It had gone on too long, Arden. The rows, recrimi-
nations. The break had to be made—clean. Not the
best way, perhaps, but didn't you ever do stupid,
unthought-out things when you were young?'

'I'm thirty-five, not in my dotage.'

'I know, but I was hurting—and it needed to end.
Didn't it?'

'Yes. And over the months the feelings faded, bitterness became indifference.'

'Yes,' she agreed. Her bitterness, his indifference.
'And now it really is too late, isn't it?'

'Yes, because we both have busy, satisfying lives—
loves.'

'Yes.' What else could she say? That she didn't have
a love? No, she had no intention of telling him that.

'We've grown too far apart,' he resumed, 'and the
Rowan I once loved no longer exists. She's all grown-
up now, and very, very tough.'

'Yes.' Tough on the outside. On the inside? She
didn't know. She needed to be but didn't know if she
was.

Stifling another yawn, she turned her head to stare
once more at the passing scenery—at long stretches of

pine trees interspersed with communities, at shopping malls, eating houses. All so different from England.

'Conversation so riveting, Rowan?' he taunted drily.

With a reluctant smile, she shook her head at him.

'Pity you missed the fall; it was truly spectacular this year,' he commented.

'Was it?'

'Yes.'

'Is that why Hetty wanted to come up?'

'Maybe.'

'Where is she—in a hotel?'

'No.'

'Renting somewhere?'

He shook his head, smiled, and she didn't know why, then, 'House,' he said laconically.

'She's *bought* a house up here?'

'No,' he denied, oh, so softly, 'I have.'

CHAPTER THREE

'You have?' Rowan whispered in shock. 'We're staying in *your* house? You didn't say it was *yours*!'

'Didn't I?'

'No! And why not? Because you knew very well—'

'You wouldn't have come if I had?' he queried smoothly.

'Yes! No! Why didn't you tell me?'

'Because I knew the reaction I'd get, and I preferred to get it when we were nearly there.'

'Knew? You don't know me at all!' she stormed.

'Suspected, then,' he purred blandly.

Her mind racing, she accused, '*You* invited her up here, didn't you? When you knew I was coming to visit, you invited her up here.'

'Now why would I do that?'

'I don't know!'

'Seems a bit illogical, don't you think? Or shall we be hypothetical? Let's say, perhaps, for my own reasons, I *wish* to play her little game.'

'What reasons?'

'She'll leave me her estate if we get back together?'

'You don't need her estate! And, anyway, she wouldn't leave it to anyone else.'

'She might. She might leave it to you.'

'Rubbish!'

'You'd probably have to stay single, of course,' he continued smoothly, 'but then, that's probably not a

42

problem. I mean, you've never found anyone else, have you?' he added, gently prodding her temper. 'Not anyone permanent, anyway.'

'Always supposing that I *want* anyone permanent. Not all women do, and how like a man to assume that a woman can only be fulfilled—'

'Not my assumption,' he cut in blandly. 'Hetty's.'

'Which seems rather curious, don't you think, seeing as *she* never married and you've just finished telling me that I would *have* to stay single?'

'If you didn't marry me, I meant. Her will will probably stipulate one or the other. And what will you answer, hmm,' he persisted, 'when she begins to ask pertinent questions?'

'What do you answer,' she asked waspishly, 'when she asks *you*?'

'Me?' he queried lazily. 'She doesn't ask me; she knows better. But you, Rowan? What will you answer?'

'That I'm perfectly happy with my life the way it is. And who said she's going to ask me awkward questions?'

'No one. We're hypothesising—aren't we?'

'Which still doesn't tell me,' she said through her teeth, why you're allowing me into your home. The same conversations, if she's insisting on having them, could have taken place perfectly well in her apartment.'

'But not with me there.'

'I don't need you there!'

'Of course not,' he agreed placatingly. 'But *she* might,' he added slyly, 'and why does it matter if it's my home or somebody else's?'

She didn't know why, only that it did.

'But not to worry,' he added softly. 'I shan't be there very much. You'll hardly notice me at all.'

'Good.'

'And you're missing all the pretty scenery,' he derided her, a laugh in his voice.

Mouth tight, she stared through the window.

'We are now in Maine,' he informed her as they crossed a short stretch of water. 'We'll do the scenic route along the coast another day.'

'Thank you,' she said tartly.

He gave a small smile. 'Over to your right is Kittery and, if you're an avid shopper, plenty of factory outlet stores.' And a short while later he added, 'The Yorks—York Village Historic District where a number of eighteenth- and nineteenth-century buildings have been restored. Cape Neddick—' he pointed '—worth going to see the Nubble Light which sits on a tiny island just offshore. Ogunquit, artists' colony. Expensive,' he added laconically.

'Should be all right for you, then,' she remarked tartly.

'Mmm.'

Turning off the 1-95 onto route 35, he said, 'Summer Street; keep looking to your left.'

Obediently doing as he said, she suddenly exclaimed faintly, 'Good grief!'

He slowed and pulled over onto the verge so that she could see it properly. 'The Wedding Cake House.'

And it was, she thought in astonishment. Fancy wood fretwork, mouldings and curves—an absolute confection set in a pretty garden.

'Apparently,' Arden explained as he drove on, 'the

sea-captain builder was forced to set sail in the middle
of his wedding and the house was his bride's consola-
tion for the lack of a wedding cake.'

'Rather sweet,' she murmured.

'Sweet?' he exclaimed with a laugh. 'Is that what
you would like?'

'Well, no, but to go to all that trouble. . .'

'The sort of trouble men go to for you?' he asked
slyly.

'I can't *help* it if men find me attractive, Arden!'

'No,' he agreed, and she looked away. She *couldn't*
help it. She didn't deliberately try to attract, wasn't
even sure why she did. She didn't think that she was
pretty—exotic, certainly, but not pretty. Odd-looking,
she always thought—a bit bizarre.

Still considering the odd effect that she seemed to
have on people, Rowan continued to stare round her
at the wood-frame houses, all in beautiful condition,
all, seemingly, set in their own grounds—well-main-
tained grounds—and she wondered why he was being
so—considerate.

She hadn't expected that he would detour to show
her places that he must have seen a hundred times. So
why was he? Because he was proud of his country?
Because he thought that she might enjoy it. But that
would mean he cared, and he didn't. He'd said so.

He'd also said a lot of other things—like not wanting
her in his country, let alone his house. . . So why had
he agreed that she should come? Why had he allowed
Hetty to make her plans? Whatever the reason, she
was going to have to cope, so she had better start
getting used to the idea.

'Is your house like these?' she asked quietly.

'Mmm. You'll like it.'

Yes, she probably would. Arden had always had excellent taste.

'I can see the sea,' she said stupidly.

'Yes. Cape Arundel. Walker's Point,' he added, 'and over there, to your right, on that little spit of land, the summer home of Ex-President Bush.'

'Fancy neighbours,' she murmured tiredly.

'Yes.'

Hellish in winter, she guessed—with the sea on either side. There only needed to be a bad storm and the house would probably get swamped. Not her problem, and presumably the ex-president liked it.

A few minutes later Arden turned off onto a narrow, tree-lined road and through a wide gateway. Set back, pale grey with white window-frames and doors, it was beautiful—nearly beautiful, she qualified, if you could ignore the ladders and the pile of broken roof tiles in an untidy pile to one side. And the builders' van, of course.

'It's not. . .'

'Ready for visitors? No.'

And then her thoughts were redirected, because to the left, beside a white picket-fence, or one that had once been white and would no doubt be again, stood a woman with long dark hair tied at her nape. She waved. His neighbour? The one Hetty didn't like? The one, Rowan knew, instinctively, that she wouldn't like either?

She had thought that he'd meant his neighbour in Cambridge. Only, of course, he hadn't. He'd meant his neighbour here. But if Hetty hadn't been up here before, how had she known about her?

Pulling up at the side of the house, he said taunt-ingly, 'Home.'

'Your home,' she corrected him.

His smile was bland.

He climbed out and courteously held the door open for her, then escorted her across the shaved grass towards the woman waiting at the fence. 'Come and meet Patricia,' he invited softly.

'Do I have a choice?'

'No,' he said. 'Rowan, meet Patricia. Patricia—Rowan.'

'Hello, Patricia,' Rowan said obediently.

'You're English,' she accused her, as though it somehow might not be allowed.

'I know.'

Arden laughed, and Patricia turned her attention to him and smiled. 'I thought I'd better warn you. I didn't know if you knew—'

'That Hetty's here?' he completed for her. 'Yes, I knew. I'll see you later.' Taking Rowan's arm, he urged her towards the house.

'At eight?' she called after them. 'Bye, darling.'

He waved one arm backwards in acknowledgement.

'Darling?' Rowan queried.

He just looked at her.

She looked back.

'I'll get your case.'

'Thank you.' Determinedly holding her smile, she mounted the three steps to the front door just as it was flung open and a young girl emerged.

'That has got to be the rudest woman I've ever met!' Dumping her bucket in the middle of the front porch, malicious satisfaction stamped clearly on her pretty face, she added bitterly, 'I hope she trips over it and breaks her neck! And if you're going in there I suggest you wear armour-plating! Do you know what she called me? "A puerile, maundering neurasthenic"! I don't even know what it *means*!'

It was nice to know that Hetty hadn't changed in the last few months. A weak heart obviously hadn't blunted her tongue. With a faint smile Rowan said, 'Well, if you can actually remember it and pronounce it you can't be as silly as she thought, can you?'

Her anger evaporating, the girl asked almost happily, 'You a Brit?'

'English.'

'Same thing, isn't it?'

'No,' Rowan replied.

'Oh. You on vacation?'

'Sort of.'

'And you want to visit the great, almighty Henrietta Lawson? Jeez. You must have rocks in your head.' The ways of the world clearly beyond her, she added, 'And if she asks I'm not coming back. Oh, hello, Arden.' She blushed.

'Mary Ann,' he greeted her, his mouth twitching just slightly. 'Having trouble?'

'Yes! She called me—'

'I heard. I'll have a word. Thank you for coming. Did you manage to finish?'

'I guess. Sort of.' She grimaced, then gave a funny little smile, sheepishly picked up her bucket, and, with a pert little swagger that set her blonde pony-tail swinging, walked off down the path and meticulously shut the gate.

'And you accuse *me* of knocking 'em dead?' Rowan taunted. 'Gee.'

'Americans do not all say "gee",' he reproved her softly.

'I know.'

'Neither are we all called Chuck.'

'I know that too.' Stepping into the hall, she stopped and stared in astonishment, because it was—derelict. Well, no, not derelict but gloomy, dusty, sad. So very neglected. Once it had probably been airy, spacious, beautiful. And could be again, with a bit of hard work—hard work that was obviously in progress if the exterior and the young lady with the bucket were any indication.

Turning, she stared at Arden's hatefully mocking smile.

'Not quite up to your impeccable standards, Rowan, but I'm getting there. But you can see, can't you, why invitations weren't actually extended?'

'All right, so I was wrong. I'm not *always* right.'

'Only most of the time? But it's quite habitable—'

'No, it isn't!' Hetty denied as she bustled through from the rear of the house.

'If you don't mind roughing it,' he finished.

'It's falling to pieces!'

'Historic,' Arden corrected her mildly. 'You came on the train?'

'Don't be silly; I hired a car and chauffeur. I expected you hours ago!'

'Ah, unfortunately we wasted rather a lot of time searching for you in Quincy Market. The question remaining, of course, is why are you here? Was it, perhaps, that you thought you should keep an eye on the builders?' he offered helpfully.

'Certainly *someone* needs to make sure you aren't being ripped off, but the truth is that I got tired of waiting.' Avoiding his eyes, Hetty glanced at Rowan— a rather searching glance, which did her no good at all, because Rowan kept her face perfectly blank.

'She's of the opinion,' Arden drawled, 'that men are quite incapable of doing anything remotely constructive.'

'And are they?' Rowan asked softly.

'Oh, yes.'

She didn't think they were talking about the house.

'*And* it's haunted,' Hetty announced.

He grinned. 'Is that a plus or a minus?'

'Don't get smart with me, Arden; just because you have about as much perception as a pepper pot and see nothing and feel nothing does not make it insignificant. Scoff all you want, but there is definitely something here. I can feel it.'

'She's into the occult,' he offered drily.

Hetty ignored him, and turning to Rowan, presented a scented cheek to be kissed. 'How are you?'

Borrowing some of Arden's blandness, she murmured, 'Fine. Just fine.' Eyeing the inappropriate black hat firmly pinned to the grey hair, she teased, 'Joined a coven?'

'No.' Still the abrupt way of speaking; still the same determination shining in those dark eyes.

'So, apart from being self-styled foreman of the building work, how are you?'

'Dying.'

'But not at this precise moment,' Arden argued

dismissively. 'I'll show Rowan to her room, and then you can show her the house. I assume you *have* toured it?'

Hetty snorted, pushed back through the door and disappeared.

'Although if there *was* a ghost,' he mused thoughtfully, 'it would only have to get a hint of her acid tongue and, if it had any sense, it would flee instantly. This way.' Indicating that she should precede him, he ushered her up the staircase. 'It's quite safe,' he added patiently when she hesitantly stepped onto the first bare stair. 'If I wanted you to break your neck, I could think up far more satisfying ways and means.'

'And do you? Wish me to break my neck?'

'No, it would cause too many complications, and I have enough of those already. First door on your left. Pretty basic, I'm afraid, but clean.'

'Thanks to Mary Anne?'

'Thanks to Mary Anne,' he agreed.

Dumping her case, he leaned in the doorway, watched her as she walked to the window and stared out. 'Why *did* you agree to come?' he asked bluntly.

'Because I like being called ma'am?' she suggested flippantly.

He grunted. '*Still* making excuses to yourself.'

'I never make excuses to myself. And I told you why I came—because Hetty said she was ill.'

He gave her a sceptical look. 'I'll see you later.'

'Well, there's an incentive,' she muttered, too softly for him to hear. And she had come because of Hetty, whether he believed it or not. No other reason would have dragged her here.

With no front now needing to be kept up, she

allowed weariness to catch up with her, let her shoulders slump tiredly and turned to survey the room. Basic, as Arden had said, but clean. The wood floor had been polished, the rug cleaned. The bed was brass, the bedding new, as were the matching curtains. Hastily obtained by Mary Ann when informed that there would be guests? The furniture was old, the wallpaper faded—and she wanted to go home.

Retracing her steps, she went to find Hetty. There was the sound of banging from somewhere above.

'There are a lot of spirits round you,' Hetty advised in her blunt way as she led Rowan towards the back of the house, before Rowan could ask what she needed to ask.

'I can hear them,' Rowan said drily. 'Why?'

'Curiosity, I expect.'

'Oh. I didn't know you were psychic.'

'Latent talent. So, how did you feel?'

'About Arden? How did you expect me to feel? Why did you do it?' Rowan asked gently. 'I was worried sick.'

'Sorry.'

'No, you aren't. Why, Hetty? You've never meddled before.'

'Does he still have the power to affect you?'

'No.'

'Liar. You should have come last year.'

Pushing open the door on her left, ignoring any answer that might be forthcoming, as she always ignored things when she'd made her point, Hetty asked slyly, 'Anyone waiting when you arrived?'

'Mmm, a tall, haughty-looking creature.'

'Patricia.'

'Yes. And is she usually waiting?'

'Yes. She has designs on Arden.'

'So he said.' But did he have designs on *her*? 'And how did *you* come to meet her? If this is your first visit. . .'

'In Boston,' Hetty said shortly. 'She positively *haunts* his offices, his home. Apparently she was up here on a visit when Arden first bought the house. . .'

'And was immediately smitten?'

'So were you, so don't deride it,' Hetty reproved her pithily.

True. 'And so you decided to throw a spanner in the works?'

'Don't do yourself down, dear. You're more in the nature of a wrench.'

With a snort of laughter, Rowan demanded only half-exasperatedly, 'And why rush up here ahead of us? You're supposed to be taking things easy.'

'You know why, and taking things easy is boring.' Turning her head, amusement glittering in her dark brown eyes, Hetty added, 'Dying is much more interesting.'

'That's a terrible thing to say!'

'Why? It's true; a whole new adventure. I'm old, tired—and you can take that look off your face; I shall be glad to go. I've been here too long. And you've become even more beautiful, if that's possible. Has maturity brought wisdom, Rowan?' she asked gently. 'Assuming, of course, that you *are* more mature.'

'I don't know. Ask me when I'm sixty.' Giving the old lady a gentle shove, Rowan pushed her into a high-ceilinged room of quite elegant proportions. A room that *had* been restored. Floor-to-ceiling windows took up the whole of one wall and obviously opened out on the wooden deck beyond. Arden was busily sounding the panelling.

'Sheet-rocked?' Rowan asked, tongue-in-cheek. She didn't know what it meant, only that she'd heard someone mention it when discussing the interior of a house.

He gave her a look of mild derision.

With a shrug, she turned to look at Hetty who appeared to be communing with her spirits. 'You really don't think he should have bought the house?' she asked.

'No. You've been here before, did you know?'

A little alarmed because Hetty normally had such an excellent memory, she looked at Arden for help, and he gave a dry smile. 'She's talking astral.'

Ignoring him, Hetty continued, 'At least three times. You have three auras.'

'Oh. Is that good?'

'I have no idea. Arden, stop trying to demolish the walls.'

His smile faint, he walked out without answering, testing the floor as he went.

'Pumpkin pine,' Hetty muttered.

'Right.' Rowan nodded without the faintest idea what they were talking about as they obediently followed the resolute Arden.

Walking through the kitchen, which was painted in institutional green, making it feel a bit like being under water, and which didn't look as though it had had anything done to it for at least a century, she nodded to a bow-legged man who was frowning over some drawings, then dallied to read the real-estate blurb which was lying on one of the surfaces.

'Terrific opportunity,' she read, 'to buy into a historical village home, featuring original woodwork—' she was sure that Arden could attest to that'—pumpkin pine floors—' ah '—cathedral ceilings. Lots of space for the whole family. 5 BRs; 2 family rooms (1 with FP); 2 dining rooms (one informal); 3.5 baths.' Three point five? What was point five? she wondered with a bemused smile. 'Set in 2.6 acre lot. Pretty views, pine trees. $385,00.' $385,000? Good heavens! Mentally calculating, although not quite sure of the exchange rate, she worked it out to be about £280,000.

The pamphlet still in her hand, Rowan walked out onto the deck, or porch—she wasn't quite sure what they called them in America. It hadn't been mentioned in the blurb. Probably because it was falling down.

'Watch your footing,' Arden warned mildly from one end.

Rowan dutifully watched her footing, and when she thought that she had watched it long enough she stared round her in delight. A dying clematis climbed unchecked across a broken support. In fact it was probably only the clematis that was keeping the support upright, but in the summer it probably looked beautiful—a profusion of flowers. 'What colour is it?'

'Pink?' he offered with clearly no idea at all.

'Hmm. Which way's the sea?'

He pointed right. 'Behind the trees.'

'Ah. What's an FP?'

He looked at her, looked at the pamphlet she still held, shook his head and carefully walked down the steps to the scrubby lawn.

Hetty also looked at her. 'Fireplace,' she explained drily.

'Ah.'

There was the sound of squealing wood, and both looked over in time to see the French windows being forced open against their obvious desire to stay shut. Arden fastidiously dusted paint flakes from his jacket.

'Rotten,' Hetty snapped.

'Warped,' he argued sweetly as Hetty carefully descended.

Standing on the lawn, she gave him a look that might have felled a lesser soul, and said reprovingly to Rowan, 'Don't lean on the railing. He won't want to be sued.'

'How much are you worth?' he asked her.

'Not enough.' Fingering the clematis, Rowan observed, 'Too late to prune, but it definitely needs tying up.'

'But not *now*,' Arden replied.

Walking carefully down the outside steps and onto the grass, Rowan joined them by the French windows. Eyes half-closed in imagining, she enthused quietly. 'Tables and chairs beneath the deck overhang. Wisteria or something on the leg; a pergola effect. The lawn relaid—'

'I'll pass on your suggestions to Patricia. You *can* come back next summer and see if they've been implemented, can't you?'

'Don't be nasty,' Hetty scolded.

He smiled and forced his way through the ill-treated French windows.

She *definitely* shouldn't have come. 'What's point

five of a bathroom?' she asked before Hetty could comment on anything else.

'No bath?' she offered.

'Ah. A cloakroom?'

'If you say so, dear,' Hetty agreed as she followed her nephew.

With a snort of weak laughter, Rowan followed her into the—what? Family room? Den? Or maybe it was a dining room. Formal or informal? she wondered. But it certainly had a fireplace. A magnificent one at that.

Trailing behind the other two—downstairs, upstairs, a brief peek into the attic, where an electrician was doing something with wires—she thought she would like to live here. Now, when it was too late, she could have lived here with ease.

'Did you really call the young lady with the bucket a maundering neurasthenic?'

'Probably.'

'Impressive. She said you were the rudest woman she'd ever met.'

'She's probably led a sheltered life.'

'Go and have a lie-down, Hetty,' Arden ordered. 'You're tired.'

For all his offhand behaviour, Rowan had been aware of how closely he'd been watching his aunt, and much to Rowan's surprise Hetty agreed. Smiling at Rowan, she said softly, 'I'm glad you came. I'll see you later.'

They both watched her walk along to her room. 'How did you find her?' he asked bluntly as he led the way back down.

'Older, tireder,' Rowan answered quietly. 'She says she'll be glad to go.'

'Yes.' He sounded indifferent, but she knew, as many others did not, that his indifference could hide concern. Not always, but sometimes, and in this instance she knew that it was the case. Hetty was the only surviving member of his family, his mother's sister. And why he had always wanted people to believe that he was hard and uncaring she had never discovered, knowing only that it was another of the many facets of his personality.

'What else did the doctor say?' she asked with a little frown of worry.

'Nothing else—just that she has a weak heart and should take care.' His eyes on hers, he suddenly grinned. 'But then, he said that years ago and she's still here to plague me. Hetty will die when she wants to die and not before.'

'Yes. Is she really into the occult?'

He snorted. 'So she says. Personally I think it's a little ploy she uses to sidetrack people when they get too pertinent.'

With a faint smile of her own, her eyes searching his strong face, and hesitating only briefly, she asked carefully, 'Were you surprised that she wanted us to meet?'

'No. We should have met before. I think I missed you.' Jumping the last two stairs, he walked along to the kitchen.

Her face a mass of comic astonishment, she stared after him. Miss her. And, even if he had, to actually admit it. . .

Holding the kitchen door open, he called, 'Come and eat.'

She nodded weakly, then gave a faint smile. 'I missed

you too,' she said softly. And she had. Missed his abrasive humour, his vitality, his—lovemaking.

'No one to fight with, Rowan?' he asked as he opened the door of the huge refrigerator in one corner and removed a large box.

'You make it sound as though I enjoyed all the fighting.'

'You did. Be honest; you enjoyed it as much as I did. Didn't you?'

A wistful look in her lovely eyes, she stared rather blankly at him. Yes, she'd enjoyed it. At first there had been an excitement, a daring about their clashes, which had usually ended in laughter, and loving. But not at the end—and you couldn't put back the clock to change the ending.

'It seems like only yesterday, doesn't it?' she mused.

'Does it? To me it seems like a lifetime. It's only cold meat and salad,' he explained as he began transferring containers from the box to the table. 'I had it delivered from the village. Tomorrow you can make yourself useful, do the shopping. Can't you?'

'If you like.'

He gave a faint smile.

'Expecting an argument, Arden?' she asked drily.

'Perhaps. Help yourself; I'll make the coffee.'

Seating herself at the table, dividing the contents of the containers between the three plates that had been set out, she asked, 'When did you move in?'

'Today.'

'You weren't actually living here at all?'

'No, just camping out when I was needed for consultation.'

'Oh.'

'Yes, Rowan, "Oh". Until Hetty decided to play whatever it is she's playing. Presumably she thought it would be more—um—intimate here, in the furtherance of her plan.'

Not wishing to comment on the plan, she carefully buttered some bread. 'I thought you were going out.'

'I was.'

'And?' she prompted, because he never, but never, elaborated on anything.

'My meeting was cancelled. Lucky, wasn't it?'

'Extraordinarily.' But he still had his meeting with Patricia to look forward to.

He made the coffee, joined her at the table, and when they had eaten, mostly in silence, and were nursing their coffee-cups he commented idly, 'Rowena de la Hay. Hard-headed businesswoman. Affluent and ruthless, determined, all energies channelled into one goal. You run your own health club, own houses you let out for an exorbitant rent. We would make a good team.'

'One house, Arden; don't exaggerate. And we never managed to pull in harness before; why suppose it would be any different now?'

'I meant a business partnership, not an intimate one. You see how wise I've become?'

'And when did wisdom, or the lack of it, have anything to do with our arguments?'

'Not often, admittedly.'

'And we're *still* on different sides of the Atlantic.'

'And you're still spoilt?'

'Wanting to stay where I was didn't make me spoilt.'

'And do you—still?' he asked softly.

'Yes,' she said firmly.

'I should never have given you the choice, should I? I wouldn't now.'

'Wouldn't you? What would you do? Stop it!' she reproved him sharply when he gave her a look that... had been special. A look that had always ended in lovemaking.

'You're blushing!' he exclaimed in delighted disbelief. 'Good God, Rowan, you surely aren't embarrassed?'

'Of course I'm not embarrassed! Don't be absurd. It's warm in here, that's all. And do you really think that taking me to bed would make any difference?'

'I don't know. Be interesting to find out, though, wouldn't it?'

'No, it wouldn't!' Wouldn't it? her mind whispered. 'And I don't know about interesting,' she continued determinedly. 'Masochistic would probably be nearer the mark.'

'Perhaps.'

Perhaps? Her eyes narrowed, she asked suspiciously, 'Need an injection of funds for the business?'

'No.'

'Then why the hypothesis? I assume it is hypothesis?'

'Of course.'

Yes, of course. What else would it have been? 'Then why?'

'No reason.'

'Arden!' she exclaimed. 'You never did anything without a reason in your life!'

'True.'

A thoughtful look in her eyes as she continued to watch him, she asked, 'Are you saying you've changed?'

'No, I'm still arrogant—and a thorough-going bastard,' he added softly as he threw back the words that she had used to him last year. 'Want to put it to the test?'

'Put what to the test?'

'Find out if we can still—turn each other on. Isn't that the current jargon?'

'No!' she denied forcefully before she could stop herself. Dear heaven, that would be inviting disaster with a capital D. She was having enough trouble with him *not* touching her; heaven alone knew what would happen if he did.

And if she'd thought for one moment that he did care she'd have—what? Been in his arms before the sentence was out of his mouth?

No, of course not. She didn't want another relationship with him. Didn't want emotion. Emotion hurt too much. And spontaneous behaviour had been burned out of her a long, long time ago. Spontaneity was punished, had always been punished, by her parents. She'd been loved if she'd conformed to what, in their opinion, was right or good, ignored if she'd transgressed.

But with Arden—that brief summer with Arden—spontaneity had been accepted, delighted in, and for a while she had been the person she had always been meant to be. But she'd paid a heavy price for it, hadn't she? The choice at the end had nearly destroyed her.

Emotion was now only allowed if it fitted in with other plans. She had fought too long and too hard for her independence—alienated her parents, and Arden—to lose it now. And yet it sometimes bothered her, this person she had become, was forced to be by her own determination.

'No,' she repeated more moderately, 'I don't want to know. I have a good life in London, a successful business. I'm happy as I am.'

'Are you?' he asked sceptically.

'Yes. And stop trying to analyse me, Arden; I'm not the same person I was last week, let alone last year.' Which was true. 'And I can't for the life of me imagine why you would want to try such a dumb experiment.'

'Can't you?'

'No.'

With a little shrug he picked up his cup. 'I was just curious, is all. You never used to be a coward,' he added tauntingly.

'Nor am I now,' she said. 'But there's a world of difference between courage and allowing myself to be dragged into a mire of your making.'

'No mire. I told you, curiosity.' Leaning back in his chair, replacing his coffee-cup on its saucer, he smiled. He looked neither friendly nor amused. 'I've watched you over the months, watched men fall like ninepins. Watched them grovel for your favours.'

'Have you indeed?' she asked with assumed interest. To her knowledge there had been neither ninepins nor grovellers, but she didn't like the thought of him having watched her. And had it been deliberate? Or inadvertent? Leaving that to be thought about later, she urged, 'Go on.'

'And I wondered how many other poor fools had had your words burned into their brain, your passion burned into their bodies, and how many were ulti-mately discarded.'

'I didn't discard you.'

'Didn't you? It felt like it.'

Astonished that he might actually be admitting to having feelings, she scoffed, 'And you want one last fling with your beautiful Rowan before taking up the cudgels with the haughty Patricia? Is that what all this is about?'

He laughed. 'Cudgels? With Patricia? She's much too refined.'

'And I'm not?'

'No. But you were exciting.'

Were? Yes, *were*, because that Rowan had been suppressed. 'And you really expect me to play?'

'Why not? You used to enjoy my lovemaking. Used to revel in it.'

'True. However, that doesn't mean I wish to again.'

His eyes were steady on her, filled with humour and disbelief, and she had to fight very hard not to react, not to let him see what his words were doing to her, because they *were* affecting her, and they mustn't.

'Then why the yearning in those lovely eyes? Why the arrogance towards Patricia? If that wasn't prompted by jealousy then it was petty, and whatever else you once were you were never petty.'

'Nor am I now. And I wasn't arrogant. I acknowledged her, didn't I?'

'Mmm.' With a slow, amused smile, he indicated her empty cup. 'Have you finished with that?'

Nodding, she replaced it in the saucer and got to her feet, as did he, and suddenly they were close together and she felt stifled. Their closeness in the car had been necessary. Their closeness now was deliberate on his part, taunting, entirely different, but if she had learned nothing else this last year she had learned how to keep her thoughts and feelings from showing on her face. It might be desperately hard but she was damned if she was going to give him that sort of satisfaction.

Widening her eyes at him, she put her hands against his chest to keep him at a distance, and even that light touch brought the flame into being—that little flare of sexual tension. Ignoring it, dampening it down, she said firmly, 'No games, Arden, I told you.'

'I didn't believe you,' he said arrogantly. Grasping her wrists, he forced her hands round to his back.

Unable to repress the little shiver of awareness, she glared at him and gritted her teeth together. Her brain and all her senses were yelling at her to get the hell out of his orbit as quickly as possible, only if she struggled he would know exactly how he could make her feel. At the moment it was only guesswork on his part, based on his own arrogance; he didn't *know*.

'Beautiful Rowan,' he murmured as his hard grey eyes stared indifferently down into hers. 'An almost tamed Rowan. I think I preferred the wildness; at least it was honest.'

'Probably, but we all learn calculation, don't we?' she said harshly. 'You more than most.'

Without answering, and with almost insulting slowness, he lowered his mouth to hers and kissed her, not roughly but with thorough mastery. And the only way to block off the sensations that were rioting through her body was to blank her mind, force it to consider mundanity—a brick wall, a pond of sludge.

She kept her lips tight shut as he tried to tease them apart, tried to touch his tongue to hers in an old, remembered game—a game that had bemused and excited her. He'd been like a drug to her then, his kisses unrestrained, hungry and disruptive. But now they were calculating, searching for a response. And if he found one he would laugh.

With a strength she hadn't known she had she shoved him away. 'Don't,' she bit out.

His faint smile was almost cruel. 'Do you know how I pictured this moment?' he asked conversationally.

'No, and I didn't know you had,' she replied stonily. 'Anyway, I don't indulge in fantasies.'

'No? Pity; it might have been amusing to compare notes,' he taunted, 'because the reality—my reality—is so far removed from my imaginings as to be laughable. All the soul-searching, all the pain. All gone, Rowan. Dead. Dead as yesterday's fire.'

'Really?'

'Mmm, really.'

Fighting to keep her breathing even, her erratic pulse caused only partly by temper, she prised his fingers loose and stepped away. 'How fortunate; now you can go to Patricia with a clear mind.'

'So I can.' With a faint, insulting smile, he flicked a finger against her cheek and walked out.

And if you cry, Rowan, she told herself fiercely, I won't ever forgive you! Her jaw clenched, she turned to stare blindly from the window.

Why? Why so cruel? He'd never been like that before. He'd sometimes been angry, mocking, indifferent, but he'd never been cruel. So why now? Because he truly did need to be sure that his feelings for her were dead and that was the easiest way of doing it? And had there really been soul-searching? she wondered. Pain? Or could everything be put down to hurt pride? Had it been for him just a blinding attraction, soon burned out?

With a long, shuddery sigh, she blinked to clear her vision. She felt a desperate need to go somewhere quiet and shake. And if she had come with him last year, what would she have been like now? Crushed and uncertain, as she had envisaged, or capable and uncaring as she now pretended to be? Or would they have worked out their differences?

Wrenching her mind from might-have-beens, she picked up her coat and walked out onto the deck. She would go for a walk, inspect the property, get some fresh air into her lungs—get her act together.

Surely a year was long enough in anyone's book to get over a man one had loved to desperation? Staring round her for a moment, she walked carefully down to the lawn, then set off in the direction of the ocean. No traffic fumes here, no sound of cars, no shouts, odours of foreign restaurants to pervade the clear air. . . Oh, don't, Rowan, she told herself. You like cities, really you do. You like the buzz and excitement, the busyness.

With another long sigh, she halted beneath an arbour that in summer was probably covered in a profusion of roses. They needed pruning—and how would you know? she taunted herself. You know nothing about roses. Didn't know anything about clematis either.

'Communing with nature?'

Swinging round too fast, she staggered and nearly lost her balance. Wrenching her arm free from Arden's quickly supporting hand, tempted to snap, she forced herself to be calm. 'No, I was just deciding that your roses needed pruning.'

'And how would you know?' he taunted easily. 'Been learning woodcraft?'

'Sure,' she agreed flippantly. 'I could probably even teach the old boy scouts a thing or two.'

'I just bet you could.'

'Like rubbing two sticks together,' she told him firmly.

'Like how to earn their merit badge?'

With a little stamp of frustration, she turned away and continued on towards the tree line that apparently hid the Atlantic.

Climbing up the well-worn path towards the edge of his property, she suddenly halted in pleased surprise. It was beautiful. Did flowers cluster on the banks in spring and summer? They looked as though they might. It looked as though wildlife might swim across the small inlet she could see.

'Nature and time have probably silted the bottom,' he murmured from beside her. 'Certainly they've eroded the banks.'

And what have nature and time done to you? she wondered. He was colder, more abrasive. Or was that an illusion? Or acting? As she was acting. A startling thought.

Glancing at him sideways, she tried to read his face—and found it impossible, as always. It had always been so very hard to know what he was thinking, feeling, because he gave so very little of himself away. That had been part of the trouble.

Making another determined effort to slough off her depression, strengthen her resolve, pretend that she had no interest in his life, she said more brightly, 'So, you're thinking of getting leg-shackled.'

'Perhaps.'

'That doesn't sound very ardent,' she reproved him. 'Poor Patricia.'

'Nothing poor about Patricia,' he denied laconically.

'Wealthy, is she? That will be nice for you.'

'Yes. Jealous?'

'Good God, no!'

'Pity. I think I might enjoy you being jealous, hurting—a twisting pain gnawing at your insides. Yes, Rowan, I think I might have enjoyed that.'

'Why? Because that's how you felt?' she asked in disbelief.

'Hell, no. I told you, I think I was glad to be rid of you.'

'So you did. And, for someone who professes to feel nothing, that sounded remarkably vengeful.'

'Vengeful?' he queried thoughtfully. 'No, you were never worth that sort of effort.'

That hurt. Dear God, how that hurt. And yet she knew what he thought of her, had always known, so why the hell did it matter? Because he sounded so indifferent? Was that it? Pride? Conceit? And if it was pride then there was even more need to wield it now.

Taking a resolute little breath that she hoped was silent, she managed almost lightly, 'Now that sounded just plain nasty. Your standards must be slipping.'

'How would you know? You never knew what my standards were. Never understood me at all. You just took what was given and then threw it back in my face.'

'Not intentionally. Not maliciously. And couldn't the same be said of you?'

'Perhaps. Easy enough to say now.'

'Yes, easy to say,' she echoed. But it hadn't been easy to do. 'I felt trapped, frightened,' she said quietly, 'and the jealousy, the rages were all part of it.'

'A grand game,' he queried, as though he had never for a moment believed anything else. 'And I never gave you reason to be jealous,' he asserted.

No, he hadn't. And how often had she told herself that she wouldn't get into pointless arguments that were so old as to be almost in mothballs? And how many times did she have to remind herself not to let him see how much she'd cared?

'Perhaps I needed to feel jealous,' she mused quietly. 'If there was cause, then there was reason. . .'

'A crazy kind of logic: if I cheated, then it was all right for you to cheat too.'

'I never cheated. . .'

'Didn't you? Not with one of the army of men I used to see arriving at and leaving your apartment?'

'I was interviewing managers,' she snapped, 'as I told you at the time!'

'So you did. But then, your idea of cheating and mine seem to differ so greatly, don't they?'

'I did not cheat!' she said angrily.

'You don't think that allowing me to believe that you would marry me was cheating?'

And what could she say to that? That she hadn't known? Hadn't thought far enough ahead?

'I didn't want a relationship with you, Arden,' she said more quietly, 'let alone anything more serious; you know I didn't. But. . .' But like snow in summer it had all been wasted effort. One touch, one look. . . 'If it had been a gentle, romantic love maybe things would have been different, but it wasn't; it was a conflagration, swamping reason.'

'And so you opted out.'

'Yes, because every time I tried to explain that I needed to prove myself first you told me not to be stupid.'

'It was stupid.'

'It was necessary!' And wasn't that just like a man? To dismiss her real reasons as—irrelevant, lump them all under the heading of stupidity?

'You arrogantly assumed you only had to say something for it to happen. I told you right at the very beginning that I didn't want a serious relationship. You didn't believe me, thought you could overrule my needs with the weight of your personality. You dismissed my wants as foolish, dismissed my plans, so was it any wonder I behaved like a spoiled child when that seemed the only way to make you listen?' she demanded passionately. 'I don't think I even believed that you really wanted me. Not me, not the person inside. I don't think you even *saw* the person inside.'

'Of course I did—and still wanted you. Against all reason, against all advice, I wanted you. A crazy madness. A summer out of time. I find it hard to believe sometimes that it all happened.' Turning his head, he added nastily, 'But you had a plan, didn't you, Rowan? Knew what you wanted—and trampled over everyone's feelings to get it. Your parents', mine. . .'

Remembering her vow, her determination never to let him see how she felt, she gave him a hard smile. 'Yes, a regular trampler.'

'And now your boots are even bigger.'

'Yes.' Because she swung away too fast, her temper as always her undoing, her foot went over the edge of the bank and she windmilled her arms backwards comically to avoid falling.

Grabbing her arm, he hauled her upright, grunted with laughter—and kissed her. Hard.

CHAPTER FOUR

'DON'T do that!' Rowan snapped, pushing Arden away,

'Why? You enjoyed it.'

'I did not!'

With the smug look of a man who knew he was right, he stared at her for some moments in silence. 'Nature can be very cruel,' he finally observed. 'Exquisite packaging with a rotten core. And don't give me that garbage about not knowing you. I *always* knew you!' Turning on his heel, he began walking back towards the house.

Not even thinking about it, she bent to pick up a clump of earth. With careful deliberation she took aim. And missed. He didn't even break stride as the clod came sailing past him. And *that*, above all, was what made him so infuriating: his refusal even to *acknowledge* that someone might be able to hit him.

'And I did not enjoy it!' she shouted childishly after him. 'All it did was emphasise my wisdom in refusing to uproot myself twelve months ago!' And he *didn't* know her! He didn't know her at all.

Feeling diminished and stupid, she gave one last glare at the view and then she too began the long walk back to the house. Surely now, after that, she would be cured?

As she passed the rose arbour she gave an idle little kick at one of the supports.

'Helpful,' someone sneered.

Her mind still on Arden, she turned in surprise and saw Patricia striding towards her. Heroically mastering a desire to attack her physically, Rowan forced herself to smile. It probably didn't look very pleasant. 'Hello. I didn't see you there.'

'So I gathered. Have a row, did you?'

So much for being polite. Turning to face the other girl fully, Rowan asked quietly, 'Does it *actually* have anything to do with you?'

'Anything that affects Arden affects me. We're very close.'

'Really? And that's why you're pacing about his grounds, is it?'

'No; not that it's any of your business, but I'm intending to landscape them for him.'

She didn't have a very nice smile, Rowan decided— cold, and sneering, but it obviously did her a great deal more good than Rowan's smile had ever done her. So what did Patricia have that she didn't? Or hadn't?

'Bully for you,' she murmured, and then, because there really seemed nothing else to say, she walked on.

And it was none of her business, was it? No. Nothing here was any of her business, except Hetty. So she would go up and see if the old lady was awake, make sure that she was all right, wanted anything to eat. And then she would go to bed before exhaustion prompted her into making any more unwise remarks.

Walking into the hall, shrugging out of her coat, she tiredly climbed the stairs. Giving a light tap on Hetty's door, she opened it and put her head inside. 'Am I disturbing you?'

'From what?' Hetty asked tartly. 'My contemplation of the ceiling?'

'Oh, well, if that's the way you're feeling. . .'

'Oh, come in!' Hetty snapped impatiently. 'Even your bad-tempered face is better than cracks!'

'I'm not bad-tempered,' Rowan argued.

'No? Been spatting with Arden? Or does that ruffled composure have another cause?'

'I don't have a ruffled composure; I just feel a bit— lost.'

'Mutinously so, judging by your face.'

'Yeah. I came to see if you wanted anything to eat.'

'Arden already brought me something.'

'Oh.' Shoving her hands into her trouser pockets, she walked across to the window and stared moodily across to the trees that hid the sea. 'Why do we do it?' she asked idly. 'Hurl ourselves at men who are sardonic, cool, remote, sometimes cruel? Why do we always find them so damned attractive?'

'Because the nice ones, the caring ones, are often boring,' Hetty commented tartly. 'Because women are arrogant little creatures who conceitedly think that they will be the one to crack the nut, find the sweetness within. When in truth there either isn't any sweetness or we break our fingers trying.'

'And which is true of Arden?'

'The latter. You have the bent fingers to prove it. You used the wrong tool, Rowan. You always used the wrong tool,' she repeated softly. 'A little bit of guile would have gone so much further—and now I think it's too late. He's grown hard.'

'He always was. . .'

'No, tough,' Hetty corrected her, 'determined, but

not hard, not like now, as though nothing matters any more. You're still in love with him, aren't you?'

From anyone else she would have resented the question, vehemently denied it. But with Hetty it somehow didn't seem to matter.

'Love? I don't know if it was ever love. Violent attraction, maybe, and those sorts of feelings can't be turned off at will, no matter how much you might want them to be.' Still staring blindly down at the grounds, she continued thoughtfully, 'If it had been love, I'd have burnt my bridges and come to the States with him. The world well lost for love, as they say.'

'And he saw you no clearer than you saw him, did he?'

'No, only the packaging.'

'The exotic flower. The bird of paradise—'

'Or parrot,' Rowan interrupted with a sad attempt at humour. 'And inside,' she sighed as she walked back to perch on the edge of the bed, 'was a sparrow, a little Jenny-wren.'

'No,' Hetty contradicted her. 'Inside was a razorbill, a Little Miss Sharp! And you made a chink in that armour of his, humanised him, then gave him his marching orders and left him vulnerable. That's what he can't forgive. Or admit.'

'But I couldn't have come, Hetty,' Rowan protested. 'Not then. We would have ended up destroying each other.'

'Perhaps,' Hetty agreed tiredly. 'And yet it started out so differently, didn't it? Dear God, I can still see the pair of you mooning sickeningly at each other— and every time I came to call during that long visit to London you were in bed!'

With a little laugh, Rowan replied, 'Not always, surely?'

'Certainly seemed like it. There was no stopping the pair of you. One look and you were in each other's arms. Or laughing about one stupid thing or another.'

'Or arguing,' Rowan put in.

'Yes, or arguing. Added spice, didn't it?'

'Yes,' she admitted honestly. Arden had been the only one ever to answer back. No sulks, no silences, just an arrogant belief that he was always right.

'And if I had known the trouble that was brewing I maybe could have done something about it—reassured you about what living in the States would be like.'

'Maybe.'

'So what happens now? You stay for a few days and then return to your exciting, busy life?'

'Don't disparage it. I work very hard.'

'But do you play?' Hetty asked pertinently. 'And if you,' she sighed, 'whom he once loved—perhaps *still* loves—can't deal with him, who the hell can? I'd do anything, you know, to help him, make him happy— even sup with the devil himself.'

'I think Arden beat you to it,' Rowan quipped not very convincingly. 'He certainly looks as though he sups with him on a regular basis, and your or even my idea of happiness is not likely to ever be his. He's like he is because he wants to be—presumably,' she added none too surely. 'And if he could hear the two of us talking he'd be furious.'

'No, he wouldn't; he doesn't seem to have any feelings left.'

'Oh, yes, he does,' Rowan insisted as she recalled his taunts. 'They might not be very good feelings but,

believe me, he does have feelings. And you're talking
as though I actually want to get back together with
him, and I don't—I can't.

'And even in the seemingly unlikely event that he
did want me back there would be resentment on my
part for having to give up my independence. And even
if he didn't make me give it up, allowed me to open a
club here, he'd want to stick his oar into it,' she
observed moodily, 'suggest improvements, tell me how
it could be more profitable, and I'd be even more
resentful, especially as his suggestions would probably
be good ones.'

'That's being rational. What about emotionally,
Rowan?'

'Ah, emotionally. That's a different ball game
altogether, isn't it? I let my emotions rule me then,
and look where that got me. No, it's best to be
rational.' No matter how much it might hurt.

'Pity; it would have been nice to see you reconciled
before I go.'

'Oh, for goodness' sake! You'll probably outlive us
all!'

'No, no, the doctor said I could go any time,' Hetty
said plaintively. 'I've had one heart attack, so a second
is most definitely on the cards.'

Giving her an old-fashioned look, Rowan retorted,
'Your acting abilities are even worse than mine! And
don't, please, die just to spite me!'

'It would make you feel guilty, though, wouldn't it?'
Hetty grinned.

'No,' Rowan denied untruthfully. Was there something in her make-up, she wondered, that invited
emotional blackmail? First her parents, then Arden,

now Hetty. Wouldn't she ever be allowed to be the person she wanted to be, needed to be?

'You're like your father,' Hetty commented softly.

'What? No!' Rowan cried in horror. 'I'm *nothing* like my father!'

'Yes, you are. Single-minded. See only one side. Your own.'

'No.' With a bitter laugh, Rowan repeated, 'No.' And wouldn't that be the final irony—to become like the person she had so busily been trying to escape? 'You don't know what he's like. No one does.'

'Except you?'

'I'm the only one who knows how he was to *me*.'

'And how was he, Rowan?' Hetty asked gently.

'Uncompromising.'

'And your mother?'

'The same.'

'Is that why you don't see them very often?'

'Yes.'

'And you don't want to talk about them, do you?'

'No.' Staring down into the old and lined face, Rowan pleaded, 'Don't make it harder. Please don't. I came because you said it was urgent, because you said you were ill. . .'

'Implied.'

'All right, implied. I love you, Hetty, worry about you, but it wasn't fair to—'

'I know, but I didn't know how else to get you here. You are so *right* for each other. It's such a waste,' she went on crossly. 'Do you have any idea how few people actually ever find that spark, a soul mate? One in a thousand, if that!'

'And you never found it?' Rowan asked gently.

'Oh, yes, I found it—and the stupid bastard died!'

'Oh, Hetty.'

'A week before the wedding,' she continued, sad, reminiscent, then gave a hollow laugh. 'He was run over by a horse and cart. Not a very romantic way to die.'

'So that's why. . .'

'Yes, that's why.' Blinking, Hetty searched the beautiful face before her, stared deep into the extraordinary eyes, grasped Rowan's hand. 'Don't you see, you foolish girl? Chances like that don't come twice. And if you don't grab them. . .' Sighing, she reluctantly agreed, 'All right, I should have known better than to interfere. Tell me what you were doing in France.'

Relieved that the soul-searching was over, sad for Hetty, sad for herself, Rowan explained, 'I'd been looking over the thalassotherapy centre near Carnac—'

'The what?' Hetty demanded comically.

'Thalassotherapy.' Rowan grinned. 'Physiotherapy methods and natural remedies.' And because it was her life, her work, and because she was passionately interested in it she began to explain more seriously to the old lady. 'Rest, relaxation, a good diet and exercise are, I think, essential to offset stress. . .'

'Stress!' Hetty castigated her. 'New-fangled words. Never had stress in my day! We didn't have time!'

'Oh, Hetty,' Rowan laughed, and, bending forward, she pressed a warm kiss to the lined cheek. 'I adore you. You're so blessedly sane!'

'*I* know that! Go on, what about this stress?'

With a faint smile, Rowan continued, 'It's very real, despite your disbelief. In fact seventy per cent of illnesses are probably caused by it. There's more pressure on people nowadays, more expected of them. More people altogether! Everyone fighting for space, fighting to get on, and sometimes people need to learn to relax, how to get the body back into rhythm.

'And more and more people are growing suspicious of drugs, wondering if they damage more than they cure, and so a vast proportion of the population are turning to natural remedies, herbs—yes, yes, I know, going back to the old ways.' She smiled. 'Well, thalassotherapy is the use of new physiotherapy methods and natural remedies, including the application of warm seawater, seaweed, mud and algae to relieve tension and anxiety. There is also a claim that it's good for rheumatism and arthritis.'

'Good grief!'

'Very relaxing, mud.'

'Did you try it?' Hetty asked with a little moue of distaste.

'Yes, of course.'

'And?'

With a grunt of laughter, Rowan confessed, 'Well, I personally didn't enjoy it; I didn't quite like the way it oozed between my toes, although I have to confess that it was great for my skin!

'But the point is that a great many people *do* enjoy it, swear it helps them. And I have to admit that the seaweed and salt-water baths were incredibly invigorating, due, apparently, to the weed found along that particular stretch of the Brittany coastline having such a high mineral content.

'Although it wouldn't be practical to have it in my fitness centre, because I'd have to transport the stuff from France, I thought I might be able to organise trips for those of my clients who *would* like to try it. I also wanted to look at their facilities for gymnastics, aerobics, sauna and massage, which I do have at my club. Oddly enough, they didn't have an aromatherapist or reflexologist. . .'

'Which are?' Hetty asked drily. 'I never did understand exactly what you did.'

'In layman's terms? Massage with aromatic oils, all with health-giving properties selected to suit the individual client. And reflexology is the manipulation of various points on the feet to improve general health, get rid of toxins.'

'Toxins? Good grief. I think I'll stick to dying. It sounds a hell of a lot easier!'

'Now be fair, Hetty; you've never tried aromatherapy or reflexology, have you? You would never let me practise on you.' She grinned.

'You practise on people who want it,' Hetty stated firmly.

'I could do it whilst I'm here,' she teased.

'You will not! You will keep your hands very firmly to yourself!'

'Or practise on me,' Arden drawled from the doorway. 'I never did get my massage with aromatic oils.'

And because she still hadn't forgiven him for his taunts or that hateful kiss she turned to give him only the glimmer of a smile. 'Buy the oils, darling, and I'll see what I can do.'

'Can I watch?' Hetty asked.

'No,' Arden said. 'It might prove too much for you. You're supposed to be dying.'

'But not at this precise moment,' Hetty argued sweetly, throwing his own words back at him.

Giving her a look of mockery, he held up the portable television he was carrying. 'As ordered. Where do you want it?'

'Don't tempt me. On the dressing table.'

He complied and, instead of leaving, collapsed into the squashy armchair beside the bed and put his feet up on the quilt. 'Tell us about your health club,' he commanded.

'Why?' Rowan asked in astonishment.

'Because we're interested, aren't we, Hetty?'

'Yes.' With mockery in her eyes, rather nastily reminiscent of her nephew's, Hetty grinned. 'Yes, do tell us all about it. And I want my full twelve months' worth.'

'You know perfectly well why, how, where and when,' Rowan reproved her.

'But not in detail. We always seem to have other things to discuss when we meet.' 'Like Arden' hung between them. 'So tell me it from the beginning.'

'No.'

'All right, then I will,' Arden offered softly.

With a rather bitter smile, because he didn't *know* anything about it, hadn't *wanted* to know anything about it when it might have mattered, and not wishing to be party to his suddenly reckless behaviour, Rowan turned away to stare once more from the window.

'She ran off to find her independence and her fortune—and discovered shelving experts and countless other poor fools who were attracted by her beauty.'

'Who's the shelving expert?' Hetty demanded.

'No one of importance, is he, Rowan?' Arden taunted. 'Just someone to be used and discarded.'

'Don't be bitchy,' Hetty rebuked him. Turning to stare at Rowan's stiff back, she asked, 'Why a health club? You were doing all right as you were, weren't you?'

'No,' Arden answered for her, 'she was working for someone else. Not to be allowed, was it, Rowan? Taking orders—when you wanted to give them?'

'No,' she agreed flatly. But the reality was sadly rather different from the imaginings.

'So why did you?' he insisted.

Moving only her head, she asked blankly, 'Why did I what?'

'Want to start a health club. You said, if I remember correctly, that it was something you'd always wanted to do. I just wondered why. And which came first—the chicken or the egg?'

'Oh, I see.' A faint, reminiscent smile in her eyes, she explained, 'Because once, a long time ago, a girl I knew dragged me along to one. It was awful. The assistants were snooty, unhelpful; they made me feel awkward, embarrassed—'

'They made *you*?' Arden queried in disbelief. '*You*?'

And there he went again, assuming that he knew her personality better than she did. 'Yes, me,' she said wearily. 'They were so damned intimidating, patronising almost, as though if you didn't dress as they thought you should, speak as they thought you should you weren't worth bothering with.

'Women don't like being intimidated by other women, don't like to feel insecure, drab, and some of those classy establishments make women terrified to

go through the door. And it—intrigued me, I suppose.
It also seemed like something I could do, something I
might like to do—and it dovetailed nicely with my
training. So I enrolled in a management and
business—'

'Management, you didn't need,' he put in mockingly.

'—course,' she continued determinedly, 'and when I
had done my training, got my certificates—'

'You began to investigate all the health clubs you
could find.'

Surprised that he *could* understand, when she had
thought that he didn't understand her at all, she
nodded. 'I pretended to be a potential member, looked
at the facilities and tried to find out what the people
were like who ran them. And they seemed all the
same. Snooty. So I began to do a little more research,
asked people I met if they would go to a health club if
it was ordinary, friendly, and in all cases the answer
was yes.'

'How were you intending to fund it?' Hetty asked
curiously.'

'Bank loan.'

'Relatively easy,' Arden scoffed, 'because the manager was smitten by her beauty.'

'Banks don't lend money on beauty,' Rowan said
flatly. But he had been smitten—and had made a
damned nuisance of himself.

'And then you met Arden,' Hetty put in softly.

Yes, then she'd met Arden. Wrong time, wrong
place, wrong everything.

When the silence in the room lengthened, became
awkward, she turned to stare at them, her chin tilted
just that little bit defiantly.

'And you had no intention of putting off your plans for—anyone. Did you?' he asked softly.

'I'd already signed a lease on the property.'

'Leases can be got out of.'

'I didn't want to get out of it,' she said tightly.

'And it took off like a rocket, didn't it?' he pronounced with a slight edge to his voice. 'All those stressed businessmen who wanted to be soothed, pump iron—'

'Pump what?' Hetty interrupted with a look of blank incomprehension.

'Iron,' Arden explained, his hard grey eyes still fixed on Rowan, 'is the current term for muscle-building, weight-training, the use of equipment to improve, they say, figures, lose weight.'

'Thank you,' Rowan retorted irritatedly. 'And it's a proven fact, not "they say". And I can't believe that you find this even remotely interesting.'

'You don't?' he queried with the bland look that always made her want to hit him. 'Why? I find it absolutely riveting to hear how our heroine overcame adversity. Rags to riches in one easy lesson.'

'I *never* had rags.' It might have been easier if she had had. Giving him a look of dislike, she returned her attention to Hetty. 'Satisfied?'

'No, but it will do to start with, although I don't for one moment believe it was as simple as you make out or Arden cynically pretends.'

'No,' Rowan agreed. And that was an understatement; it had been damned hard work—harder than it needed to have been, because Arden had been so difficult about it all. And then, when the rift had grown too wide, there had been the compulsion to keep busy, to try and forget the trauma of her break-up with him, to try and come to terms with the fact that she missed him like hell, that her nights were cold and lonely. But not his. Because he had Patricia, didn't he?

'How long are you intending to stay?' Hetty asked.

'A few days.'

'Make it a week,' she said temptingly.

'Good heavens, no,' Arden interjected with hateful derision before she could answer. 'She has an empire to run. Don't you?'

Ignoring him, Rowan bent to kiss Hetty's cheek. 'I'm going to turn in; I can barely keep my eyes open. Take care of yourself.'

'Why?' Hetty demanded with a trace of cynicism.

'Oh, don't you start!' Feeling hurt and incredibly tired, she straightened. 'Shout if you need anything.'

'I will. We'll talk properly tomorrow.'

'Yes, of course.'

'So long as Arden's not here,' Arden put in softly with a rather taunting smile.

Eyeing him, Rowan copied his smile. 'On the contrary, I suddenly find I don't give a damn whether you're here or not.' And at that moment she actually believed that she meant it.

Arden caught her up on the landing a few seconds later. 'Don't go to bed in a temper,' he cautioned. 'You won't sleep.'

With a long sigh, she halted, gave him an aggravated glance. 'I'm not in a temper, just. . .'

'A little bit muddled?' he asked helpfully.

'Tired,' she corrected him. Confused by his nearness, his sudden concern—however spurious it might be— she whispered, 'Will she be all right? She seems so. . .'

'Bitter? Is it surprising? She was always so active, always going off on her travels. Postcards from exotic places. And she finds it so hard, this curtailment of her lifestyle, not being able to do all the things she once took for granted. You'll stay the week? As she asked?'

Ah, so that *was* why he was being nice. Fool, she berated herself, to have even briefly thought that he hadn't wanted her to go. 'Maybe. I'll see.'

Moving on towards her room, she was surprised to find him following. Surprised and a little alarmed. Hands shoved into his trouser pockets, and with a nod that was almost dismissive, he ordered, 'Sleep well.' And then he grinned. 'Not that you will.'

'I'll sleep perfectly well, thank you.' If he thought that dreams of him would keep her awake. . .

'You really ought to stay up as late as you can, you know, otherwise you're likely to wake at five.'

'Nonsense. Why would I wake at five?'

'Because your body clock is wrong. Just a tip from a constant traveller.' With a mocking smile, he added, 'I'll see you in the morning.'

'But not at five,' she argued determinedly.

Moving past her, he opened her door, then walked across to draw the curtains. Finding the cord, he halted, stared down out of the window and smiled. An open invitation if Rowan ever saw one, but if she didn't go to look she would keep wondering what he'd been smiling at. Moving to his side, she too stared down, and saw Patricia standing on her side of the dividing fence. 'Your beloved is obviously waiting to speak to you. Best not keep her waiting. No doubt she wishes to invite you for afternoon tea or something. That *is* what country people do, isn't it?' And she tried very hard not to sound bitter, but sadly didn't succeed.

His eyes narrowed on her beautiful face and he suddenly gave one of his wolfish smiles. 'Yes, Rowan, it's what country people do, although it's a little bit late for afternoon tea.'

'There's always tomorrow.'

'Yes,' he agreed, 'there's always tomorrow.' And then, to her utter astonishment, he began to laugh. Leaning one arm against the frame, his face full of warmth and amusement, he repeated softly, 'Afternoon tea. Remember?'

With a frown, she shook her head.

'You must do! Just after we met. . .'

'The picnic!' she suddenly exclaimed. 'Afternoon tea!' With a laugh of her own, she said slowly, 'Do you know, I'd forgotten all about that? Soggy paste sandwiches, a bottle of wine. . .' And for a moment—a beautiful, brief moment—it was just as it had always been.

'And geese! Lord, I think that was the funniest thing I've ever seen.'

'Well, who on earth would have suspected that geese simply adore soggy paste sandwiches?'

'And they chased you all along the lake. . .'

'Until my hero rescued me.' He'd swept her up in his arms, laid her gently back on the rug, and, with the sunlight dappling through the leaves of the overhanging tree, he'd kissed her—gently at first, and then with growing passion. Such a good, beautiful day that had been. The smile in her eyes dying, she said softly and a little sadly, 'I bet Patricia doesn't make paste sandwiches.'

'No,' he agreed gently. 'And coffee instead of Earl Grey tea.'

'And no geese.'

'No, definitely no geese.' And then, in an action as unexpected as it was poignant, he bent to kiss her cheek. 'Get some sleep. I'll see you in the morning.'

'Yes,' she whispered. Knowing that she was about to make a fool of herself, she watched him walk to the door and quietly close it. Afternoon tea. With Patricia. Deliberately refusing to wait and watch him as he walked towards the boundary fence, she blinked away silly tears and went to get ready for bed.

She woke at five. Exactly at five. On the dot. And heard Hetty knocking.

CHAPTER FIVE

SCRAMBLING from the bed, her red hair wild, and in a Pooh Bear nightshirt, Rowan hurried along the landing and pushed open Hetty's door. 'Hetty?' she whispered softly.

'Oh, Rowan, I don't feel very well,' Hetty breathed, and she sounded so lost, so sad, so—pathetic.

Alarmed, because Hetty *never* sounded pathetic, she walked quickly across to the bed and took the old lady's hand—a hand that felt damp, trembling. And in the soft light from the bedside lamp Rowan saw how grey she looked.

'I was floating,' Hetty explained, as though still very perplexed by it all, 'all away from my body, and I knew that if I didn't get back I would die.'

'Oh, Hetty. I'll get Arden!' Rowan exclaimed hastily. Gently patting the hand in a gesture of comfort, and feeling useless and frightened, she laid it back on the coverlet and hurried out to find Hetty's nephew. Worried sick, not knowing which room was his, she flung open all the doors along the landing until she saw him, already up, one long leg into a pair of jeans, chest bare. She began, 'Hetty—'

'I'm on my way. Bad?'

'I think so.'

'Ring for an ambulance; number's on the pad by the telephone in the hall. Make sure they know who it's for.'

Nodding, she hurried to obey. Had he been waiting for just such a call? Heard her get up?

Jumping the stairs two at a time, she went down to the hall and found the number, quickly punched out the digits, took a deep breath and calmly explained—and then didn't know the address. She panicked momentarily but the soothing voice at the other end calmed her, asked the name, and then it was all right because they obviously knew about Hetty. Had they been alerted by Arden when he'd found out that his aunt was coming to stay?

Replacing the receiver, she hurried back to Hetty's room. 'Five minutes,' she whispered breathlessly. 'How is she?'

'I don't think it's another attack,' he said softly. 'Probably overdid things yesterday.' He was perching on the edge of the bed, Hetty's frail hand held in his larger one; he was smiling down at the old lady, gently chiding, and in that moment it was as though Rowan still loved him, saw him as he could sometimes be—gentle, caring—warm. Her heart turned slowly in her breast, and she wanted to go to him, encircle that strong back with her arms, be a comfort. Fool, such a fool.

Shivering a little, she wrapped her arms round her own waist instead and waited, eyes worried. 'They won't be long,' she repeated, trying to comfort herself, perhaps, as much as anyone, and then heard the swish of tyres on the damp road.

'I'll go,' Arden said as he rose easily to his feet, and, just as Rowan had done, gently patted the hand he still held before placing it back on the covers. 'Soon have you safe.' With a last smile, he walked out, not running

as Rowan had done but his long strides quickly cover-
ing the distance to the bedroom door, and she heard
him running lightly down to open the front door.

'I'm sorry to be a nuisance,' Hetty murmured.

'Don't be silly; just get better; that's all that matters.'

'Yes. I don't really want to die.'

'I know,' Rowan said softly as she took Arden's
place on the bed. 'Don't talk; save your energy and
you'll be up and about in no time at all.'

'Yes. Rowan,' she began again urgently, 'if—'

'Shh.'

Managing a smile, and in a voice that was papery
thin, Hetty confessed drily, 'I'm not really psychic.'

'Aren't you?' Rowan asked gently.

'No, but I do think I had an out-of-body experience.'

'Oh, Hetty.' And then the medics were there—
competent, kindly. Arden appeared behind them hastily buttoning a shirt.

'I'll go with her; I don't know how long I'll be. Field
any calls, will you?'

'Yes, of course. Can't *I* come?' And then she realised
that they needed to go now, not wait until she'd
dressed. 'No, you go, but you'll ring? Let me know. . .?'

He nodded, and then Hetty was being carried downstairs to the ambulance, an oxygen mask over her face.
She looked little, unfamiliar, and Rowan swallowed a
lump in her throat. She'd be all right—of course she
would.

Standing on the step, Rowan watched as Hetty was
loaded into the ambulance, watched Arden climb in
beside her. Shivering in the early-morning air, arms
still hugged round herself for comfort, she waited until

the ambulance had driven out through the gate and disappeared, before finally going back inside.

The workmen arrived at eight and she was still in her nightshirt, still cradling a cold cup of coffee, her eyes almost blank, and Arden still hadn't rung.

You're pathetic, she told herself. Go and get dressed. Hurrying up to her room, she showered, dressed in jeans and a warm sweater and then returned to the kitchen. Making fresh coffee for herself and the workmen, forcing herself to eat a piece of toast, she walked into Arden's study and shut the door.

He rang half an hour later, said that he would be back in an hour and that Hetty was resting comfortably.

When he did return, his mood was far from friendly.

'Did the workmen turn up?'

'Yes, they... You must have seen their van! How—?'

'Not those workmen! The ones to do the kitchen!'

'Oh, no. How's—? Arden!' she snapped when he turned away to pick up the phone, began punching out numbers. 'How's Hetty?'

'Hetty's fine,' he said impatiently. 'They're keeping her in for a few days... Hello? Ryan? Where the hell are your men?' He listened and his face hardened. 'Yes, they'll get paid,' he stated grimly. 'No, I'm not,' he said to whatever query had been put. 'Then make sure they are.' Putting the phone down, he stalked across to the front window.

'What was that all about?' she asked curiously.

'Nothing,' he replied tersely.

'But it sounded as though—'

'Leave it!'

With a little sigh, she asked instead, 'Was it her heart?'

'No. Yes. I guess,' he added wearily, then gave a grunt of very unamused laughter. 'She was supposed to be taking it easy—and running round Boston definitely didn't come under *that* heading. But if the damned doctor thinks *I* can keep her under control without actually tying her to a chair. . .'

'How long will she be in the hospital?'

'I told you, a few days. What's the matter? Afraid of being alone with me?'

'No.'

But he wasn't listening; his eyes were on the truck pulling into the drive. 'About time too,' he muttered. Striding past her, he walked along the hall and wrenched open the front door to admit, presumably, the kitchen workmen. Who were late. And who seemed to think that they might not get paid. Curious. And what was she supposed to do whilst all this activity was going on? Twiddle her thumbs?

Needing action—any action—to get over her earlier worry and fright, she grabbed her coat from the hall and decided to go for a walk. At least the rain had stopped. It wasn't even very cold, just blustery.

The pile of slates had gone from the front garden, she saw. She was glad that she didn't work for him; she doubted if he was a very easy taskmaster. But she didn't think that he had ever not paid anyone.

With a shrug, knowing that he wouldn't tell her even if she persisted, she took a route at random and eventually found herself at a small rocky bay, which was probably tranquil in the summer. Perching on a convenient boulder, she watched the waves crash and

gently retreat, crash and retreat, and allowed spume to
mist her hair. It was really rather soothing. Sea birds
wheeled and screamed, and in the distance a boat
trundled, seemingly unhurriedly, across the horizon.

And just what, she wondered, had put Arden in such
a foul mood? Apart from the kitchen workmen.
Because Hetty was worse than he'd said? Because the
doctor had given him a hard time? Or had it been
guilt? Although it was hard to see how he could have
prevented his aunt running round Boston on her own.
A very determined lady, was Hetty. But not today.
And she herself was supposed to be going shopping,
wasn't she?

She stayed for about an hour, then slowly made her
way back by a different route, tried to imagine how
the trees had looked in the fall. A few red leaves still
clung to baring branches and a scent of woodsmoke
drifted to her nostrils. And although the sky was grey
the air felt crisp, clear. A nice place, a good place, a
place that felt—friendly.

She came across a little village—well, a craft shop, a
general store and a small hotel—and then walked
slowly back to the house—where bedlam reigned.
There was no sign of Arden. Perhaps he was shut up
in his study. Perhaps he'd run away.

The kitchen was now non-existent, just filled with
chaos—equipment being ripped out, equipment being
installed, a painter trying to paint, a plumber trying to
plumb. And so she wandered into the formal—or
informal—dining room, sat at the table that now
resided there—just plonked down, presumably, until
someone found a permanent home for it. A nice
table. Antique.

The little click of the French window opening behind
her made her jump. Someone had obviously unwarped
it, shaved the edges—but not, she thought, the grey-
haired man with the twinkling blue eyes who was
regarding her. Tall and slim, in his sixties, he came
fully into the room, closed the door carefully behind
him and then just continued to stare at her.

'Good Lord!' he exclaimed weakly. 'Are *you*
Rowan?'

'Yes.'

'Oh, my, oh, my, oh, my.' His lips twitched, and then
he burst out laughing.

'And you are?' she asked with an aloof little toss of
her head.

Sobering, or at least trying to straighten his face, he
introduced himself solemnly. 'Patricia's uncle.'

'Oh.'

'Yes.' His mouth still fighting its grin, he continued
blandly, 'She's staying with me.'

'Ah.'

'Comes whenever—'

'Arden's here. Yes, I know.'

'Mmm. She didn't say. . . Well, she wouldn't, would
she?' he asked comically. 'Only, of course, I now
understand why she took an instant dislike to you.'

'The feeling, I assure you, was mutual.'

He grinned. 'Such *fierce* competition.'

'So they say.' She was a threat to any woman with a
man. She could never imagine why it didn't occur to
these stupid women that she didn't *want* their wretched
men! Only, of course, in Patricia's case that simply
wasn't true, was it? Fighting to keep her own face from

showing her feelings, she waited, widened her eyes at him.

He chuckled. 'And you'd feel the same way about anyone who showed an interest in Arden?' he guessed with a perspicacity she could have done without.

'It did sound remarkably like sour grapes, didn't it?' she queried pleasantly, but there was an edge to her voice that didn't go unnoticed.

'A little. And may I say that you have to be the most astonishingly beautiful woman it has ever been my pleasure to meet?' Thrusting out his hand, he said, 'Thomas A. Brown. Or just good old Tommy Brown to my friends.'

'Hello, good old Tommy Brown. And may *I* say that you are a vast improvement on your niece?'

'Thank you,' he acknowledged drily. 'And you look remarkably fed up.'

She sighed. 'Yes, and worried, and feeling rather like a spare part. Hetty's ill.'

'Oh, I'm sorry. Patricia said she was here.'

'She's in the hospital. All right, I think, but. . .'

'You now find yourself at a loose end?'

'Something like that.' There was a loud crash from the kitchen and they both grimaced.

'First time in the States?'

'Mmm.'

'Then how about,' he began as he hooked out the chair opposite with his toe and sat down, 'I take you sightseeing? I have to go into Freeport this morning. . .'

The door opened and Arden looked in. 'Oh, there you are!' he stated accusingly. 'I've been looking all over for you.'

'Me?' Tom queried comically.

'No! Rowan!'

'I went for a walk,' she said shortly.

'Well, thank you for letting me know. Tom, I need a word. Ryan seemed to think—' Breaking off, he glared, then added, 'We can talk in my study. When you've finished here, of course,' he added pickily.

'Oh, my,' Tom said softly with an infectious chuckle as Arden went out. 'Blows the wind in that quarter? Poor Patricia.'

'Don't,' Rowan warned, 'jump to conclusions.'

'Not even when they leap down my throat?'

'No.'

'Fair enough. Freeport? Yes? No?'

'Yes. Thank you.'

'Ten minutes.'

She nodded, and when he'd joined Arden she went upstairs to get ready. If Arden still needed shopping, no doubt Tom would be kind enough to tell her where to go. Even help her do it.

Feeling defiant and wretched, she exchanged her jeans for tailored grey trousers, knotted a pretty scarf at her neck, lightly made up her face, collected her bag and returned downstairs. Tapping on the study door, she poked her head inside. Arden was behind his desk, Tom at the window.

'Am I interrupting?' she asked stiffly.

'No.' Arden replied. 'And there's no need to sound peevish.' He sounded even more peevish than she did.

'I wasn't aware I did. You said something about shopping. Tom's offered to drive me into Freeport. I'd also like to visit Hetty.'

Leaning back in his chair, he steepled his fingers

under his chin and stared at her. Tom turned, gave a half-smile, blue eyes twinkling with dangerous delight.

'Mary Ann can do the shopping, and Tom knows where the hospital is.'

She nodded and withdrew. Bastard.

Tom joined her almost immediately, amusement still writ large on his mobile face, and because he was doing her a favour, because she actually quite liked him she apologised. It was still stiff, still aggravated, but an apology nevertheless. 'I'm sorry. I didn't mean to be rude.'

'Didn't you?' he laughed.

Staring at him, she gave a rueful smile. 'Yes. I did.'

'But not now?'

'No.'

'Good. Can I ask an impertinent question?' he murmured as he gently took her arm and urged her through the front door.

'You can ask; I won't necessarily answer.'

'I know that you're Hetty's god-daughter, but you and Arden. . .?'

'Were once more than friends? Yes. How far is it to Freeport?'

'Not far; the other side of Portland,' he explained in amusement. 'And could be again?' he persisted softly.

'No,' she said unequivocally.

With a little chuckle, he led her next door, helped her into his large car, and Rowan sighed. 'It's a subject with too many thorns to pick through,' she added, perhaps in mitigation—she didn't know. She didn't feel as though she knew anything any more.

Thankfully, Tom probed no more and she slowly relaxed. He was a comfortable man to be with. He had a delightful sense of humour, kindly pointed things out to her, chatted easily about his new and thoroughly enjoyable retirement from a law firm, coaxed information from her about her club, and by the time they reached Freeport Rowan felt as though she had known him for years.

'And I didn't see a moose,' she said sadly.

'And you quite yearn to?'

'Yes. I keep seeing signs but no moose.'

'Perhaps on the way back.'

'Yes.'

'Lunch first, I think. The Corsican. Ever had clam chowder?'

She shook her head.

'Want to try it? With fresh, home-baked bread?'

'Please.'

The little restaurant was packed and obviously popular, and they were shown upstairs to a small table in the window where a delightful young lady, very reminiscent of Mary Ann, served them.

'Good?' Tom queried when she'd finished the chowder.

'Mmm, different. And now I have to try the blueberry pie.'

'You've never had blueberry pie?' he exclaimed in scandalised accents.

'Nope. Blackberry, raspberry but never blue, although I believe Harrods sells it.'

'But not like this.'

'No, probably not like this.'

When they'd finished, were thanked for their custom and told to have a nice day, Tom led her up Mechanic

Street and into the famous L. L. Bean store. 'Would you prefer to wander on your own?'

'Yes, please,' she said gratefully.

'Then let me get you a map of the village.' Taking one from the circular desk in the entrance, he opened it and explained, 'It lists all the shops, factory outlets, candlemakers—you name it, we got it.' He smiled. 'And I'll meet you back at the car when you've finished. No hurry; take all the time you want. I'll be able to see the car from where I'm meeting with friends, so no need to feel guilty if you're a long time.'

'Thank you.'

He grinned, waved and walked away.

Freeport was delightful. Wonderful little shops, delightful people. No one made her feel guilty for just browsing and everyone asked how she was, and often looked slightly startled when she told them, so she listened to what other shoppers answered and then followed suit.

Her English accent was remarked on with delight, and she didn't think that she had *ever* spent a more enjoyable day. Quilts, ribbons, soap and candle outlets, handbags, sweatshirts—and a moose. Six inches high, furry, stuffed, in his own little knitted jumper and with the most adorable quizzical expression on his face.

Calvin Klein, Ralph Lauren, Donna Karan. She bought some lawn handkerchiefs for Hetty, a little knife that did everything from digging out stones from horses' hooves to filing your nails for Tom as a thank-you for bringing her. She debated buying something for Arden, and then didn't because she didn't know what to get, couldn't see anything silly or funny that might amuse him. Once she would have, but not today, and that, somehow, seemed the saddest thing of all.

Tired, laden, feet aching, she finally made her way back to the car at gone five. Tom was there in minutes, his smile wide, and it grew even wider when he saw the well-dressed moose sitting smugly on top of her shoulder bag.

'Morris,' she explained with a tired smile. 'I couldn't resist him.'

'Nor much else,' he observed, 'judging by the parcels.'

'No. I've had a lovely time.' But not long enough. Not nearly long enough.

'Good. We'll pop in and see Hetty and then go home.'

Except that it wasn't home, although it was blessedly silent. Remembering that she hadn't rung her club to let them know where she was and give them the number so that she could be contacted, she did that, then took her parcels up to her room.

Returning downstairs, she was unable to find Arden, but the lights were on so she assumed he hadn't gone far. She wandered into the kitchen and halted in astonishment. Gone were the green walls; gone was the old-fashioned equipment... They must have worked like demons!

And then she saw Patricia mounting the steps to the deck and grimaced. Remembering the kindness of her uncle, Rowan determined to be nice. Or at least polite.

'Hi,' she greeted her when Patricia opened the back door. 'I was just about to make some coffee; would you like some?'

'No, thank you. Where's Arden?

One, two, three, four, five... 'I don't know. I've only just come in. He's maybe gone to visit his aunt. He was quite worried about her.'

'Don't be absurd,' Patricia said dismissively. 'She's a foolish old woman who's been sponging off him for years. I should think he'd be glad of a rest from her. Visitors dumped on him when he has so much to do...'

'She doesn't sponge off him! Hetty doesn't need to sponge off anyone!' Her lovely face shocked, Rowan exclaimed, 'You really think he doesn't care? Can you really be that lacking in understanding? Don't you know him at *all*?'

'Of course I know him! Obviously a great deal better than you do! Now stop being so obstructive!'

Obstructive! She wasn't being obstructive, but, hateful as the thought might be, perhaps Patricia did know him better, understand him more than she had ever done. 'I truly don't know where he is. Maybe he wanted to be alone for a bit.'

'Alone from you, perhaps, not from me! No—'

'For pity's sake, Rowan!' Arden exclaimed from behind her. 'You've only been back in the house five minutes and already you're causing discord!'

With a squeal of alarm, she swung round. 'Do you have to creep up on people?' she snapped.

'I wasn't aware I had. Touchy, aren't you?'

'*Me* touchy? And I was not causing discord. I merely said I didn't know where you were!'

'You didn't look very far. Yes, Patricia, you wanted me?'

'Yes,' she said softly, a gentle smile on her face that made Rowan want to throw up. 'Although if left to your—er—guest I wouldn't have found you at all. I've had some ideas for a summer house.'

'Make it a gazebo,' Rowan encouraged pithily, 'and Arden might be interested. Mightn't you, dear?' she asked sweetly. 'Arden *likes* gazebos.' Pushing past him, she walked out.

'A bit prickly, isn't she?' she heard Patricia comment.

Not waiting to hear what Arden replied, because it would probably be something she didn't want to hear, Rowan walked slowly along the hall. And if Patricia thought *that* had been prickly she must have met some very funny hedgehogs!

The phone rang just as she walked past it and she snatched it up without thinking. 'Yes?' she demanded bluntly. 'Oh, hello, Sue. No, no, everything's fine.' Fine? Oh, yes, really brilliant. She explained to her secretary that she had only rung earlier to leave the number and added, 'I should be back in a few days.'

'Is that for me?' Arden asked from behind her.

Replacing the receiver, she said stiffly, 'No. It was the club.'

'Secretary run off with the petty cash, did she?'

'No, she didn't!' Twitching away, she moved to the staircase, only to be brought to a halt by his heavy palms descending onto her shoulders.

'Stop being difficult,' he reproved her as he turned her round. 'It was meant to be a joke.'

'Ha, ha—and I did not try to stop Patricia from finding you!' she added crossly.

'I don't suppose you did. You didn't really expect her to *like* you, did you?'

'Why shouldn't she? I haven't done anything to her. In fact I've been remarkably restrained!'

'Mmm, remarkably.'

'Oh, I'm going up to make my bed.'

'Mary Ann will have done it.'

'Then I'll go up and inspect it!'

His little snort of laughter was hardly guaranteed to restore her equilibrium. She didn't even know why she was cross. Not really. Yes, you do, she told herself mutinously as she climbed the stairs; you're peeved because Arden took Patricia's side against yours.

Did he like Patricia because she was the complete opposite of herself? Or were there a few hidden qualities in his haughty neighbour? Must be bloody well hidden, then; that was all she could say!

With a bewildered little sigh she walked into her room. And that was even more depressing. What was she intending to do? *Hide* here? And getting upset was stupid and irrational, she told herself forcefully. Neither Arden nor Patricia was worth it. Well, Patricia wasn't, anyway.

Feeling all churned up and twitchy, she gave a funny little half-smile as she decided that what she needed was to follow some of the advice she gave her clients— do a few calming exercises. She wasn't sure that they would work but they were better than standing here getting more and more fed up.

Deliberately blanking her mind, refusing to think any more, she sat on the floor and dragged off her boots and socks—and saw with horror that her feet were a funny colour, all red and blotchy. And swollen. Oh, hell—the flight, she supposed; she vaguely recalled someone telling her that feet sometimes swelled on a long flight. Not much that she could do about it, presumably, but they didn't look very nice.

Lying supine on the floor, she closed her eyes and slowly and deliberately untensed her muscles, concentrated on her breathing, concentrated on drawing air into her lungs, holding it, letting it out slowly. Her mind centred only on her breathing, she gradually felt calmness and strength return. It might only be a spurious calmness but hopefully it would enable her to cope with Arden. Arden who seemed to be deliberately trying to wind her up.

She heard the door open and she tensed. Heard it close and warily opened her eyes. Arden was standing there, watching her. He was wearing his mocking smile, and that made it easier. 'What do you want?' she asked rudely.

'A massage?'

'Very funny.' Pulling a face, determined not to be provoked any more, she got slowly to her feet. 'Your beloved gone, has she?'

'Mmm.'

'So you decided that a bit of Rowan-baiting would relieve your boredom?'

'No, I came to see if you were all right. You seemed. . .upset.'

'Irritated,' she corrected him.

'And is the bed made to your liking?'

'The bed's fine.'

'Perhaps I'd better try it out.' With a wicked smile, he walked across to it and lay down. 'God, I feel as though I've been run over by a truck.'

'Must be getting old,' she said derisively. 'And if anyone could be called prickly,' she added without really intending to say any such thing, 'then Patricia could.'

'She doesn't like being shouted at,' he murmured blandly.

'Then you're not going to have a very satisfying liaison, are you,' she retorted, 'seeing as shouting is an integral part of your nature?'

'Only when I'm near you,' he returned softly.

She didn't believe that. She was beginning not to believe anything he said. Watching him warily as he settled himself more comfortably on the bed, she wondered what game he was playing now. In the last few hours he'd run her through every emotion it was probably possible to feel.

'How was Freeport?' he asked.

'Fine.'

'Certainly you seem to have bought up half of it,' he commented as he nodded towards the carrier bags stacked in the corner. 'Who's the moose for?'

'Me.'

'Getting broody, Rowan?'

'No. I've always liked soft toys.'

'Mmm, and you know what they say about women who collect them, don't you?'

'No,' she replied stonily.

He gave a bland smile. 'That they're emotionally deprived.'

'Only in America,' she returned sweetly. 'And Americans psychoanalyse everything.'

'It makes us better people,' he asserted. 'Tom still in one piece, is he?'

'Yes.'

'And did you have time in your hectic schedule to visit Hetty?'

'Yes.'

'And how did you find her?'

'Fine.'

Unexpectedly, he chuckled. 'Don't want to play, Rowan?'

'No.'

'You've changed,' he commented idly.

'Have I?'

'Mmm. The Rowan I once knew always wanted to play.'

'She got cured,' she said shortly.

'Rubbish,' he declared dismissively. 'You can't so radically change your nature.'

'It's not rubbish,' she argued. 'And I can change as much as I want. I'm a better person now,' she insisted, more for her own benefit than for his. 'More fulfilled.'

'Implying that you weren't happy with yourself as you were? Why? Why did you hate being what you were so much?'

Dragging her eyes away from the disturbing length of him, she leaned back against the dressing table and tried to bend her mind in a different direction—as she was always trying to do with this man. 'I didn't hate what I was,' she began slowly. 'I hated not being able to control things—I told you.'

'But to try to change so radically, damp down the temper that's an integral part of you, play the efficient businesswoman. . .'

'Not play,' she corrected him. 'I am efficient. Capable, calm—usually,' she added with a little grimace.

'Except when you're near me,' he murmured.

Not sure if he was being deliberately provocative or merely playing tit for tat, she considered how to answer, but as he put his hands beneath his head and crossed his ankles another emotion began to intrude.

That pose, on another bed, not so very long ago, had been one he had used when he had insisted that she be the instigator in their lovemaking. When she had teasingly stripped for him, stripped him in turn. . .

Feeling warmth flood through her, she turned away—she hoped casually—to rearrange the few pots on the dressing table, but she had to wait a few moments to regulate her breathing before she could agree. 'Yes, except when I'm near you. You're the one person who has the ability to wind me up, goad me.'

'And has no other man dragged you fighting to the edge of emotion, Rowan? Has no other man in all these months found the core of your needs?'

'Goading isn't the core, and there haven't been any other men.'

'Haven't there? Then you must be feeling damnably frustrated!'

As he was? Or had Patricia already eased those needs? Mentally blocking out a thought that she did *not* want to contemplate, she wondered instead why he continued to be so stupidly insistent on the subject of other men. Because it bothered him?

'I'm not in the least frustrated,' she said. 'I live a busy and satisfying life.'

'Because men don't understand your needs?' he mocked. 'But then, you don't understand your own needs, do you, Rowan?'

'I understand my needs very well.'

'Do you? I strongly doubt it.' With a little sigh, he continued absently, 'It's funny, isn't it? Chemistry, I suppose. I can dislike you, dislike all you now stand for, have no loving, warm feelings, and yet can still admire your looks—and want to take pleasure in your body. And perhaps if you'd had a violent love affair it would have cancelled out your feelings for me.'

Would it? She somehow doubted it—and she didn't want a violent love affair. Don't you, Rowan? she taunted herself. Do you want just a nice, safe, gentle love? How unutterably boring. But boring was—safe. 'Perhaps I never had any strong feelings for you,' she offered. 'Perhaps all it ever was was infatuation.'

'Infatuation?' he queried softly.

She gave him a quick glance and looked hastily away. Sardonic, ruthless Arden—and he made her heart beat just that little bit faster, evoked erotic visions, dreams. Why? Why this man above all others? On a rational level such feelings were foolish, so why couldn't she be rational? He had hurt her unbearably—no, she had hurt herself because the choices had been so hard. And why was he here, speculating? Because he was worried about Hetty? Needed a distraction from his feelings?

And he lay on her bed, his strong body seemingly relaxed, his long legs crossed at the ankles, his grey eyes steady, as though he had all the time in the world to discuss philosophy. As though she were no one, as though nothing would ever have any effect on him again. There appeared to be no warmth in him, no passion. Was he passionate with Patricia?

Hastily shutting off that damned silly thought, she said quickly, 'Well, maybe that's what it was. I don't think it could be called love. Loving is giving, caring. . .'

'And all you gave me was a hard time.' Rolling easily to his feet, he went to stand at the window, presenting an indifferent back. 'Oh, I loved you, Rowan,' he said quietly. 'Heart and soul. It wasn't a feeling I trusted very much, but yes, I loved you.'

'In your way,' she couldn't resist adding.

Turning only his head, he looked at her without expression. 'What other way is there?'

'No other way,' she agreed. 'No other way at all.' When he resumed his contemplation of the view outside, she stared at him, at his straight back, at the grey hair that brushed against his collar, the broad shoulders—shoulders that she had once bitten into in passion, and need. 'And then was there hurt, Arden?' she asked. 'Then hatred? And then indifference?'

'Not even that,' he murmured. 'There seems to be nothing.' Turning again, he gave her a twisted smile. 'Why the need to know? Afraid I might try to seduce you?'

'No,' she denied hastily. 'Mere curiosity.'

'Makes a change. Once upon a time you would have reached for the scissors, tried to add a few more scars to my collection.'

'And to hear you speak anyone would think I'd spent the whole of our—liaison trying to injure you!' she retorted indignantly.

'Didn't you? It sometimes seemed like it.' With a more genuine smile, he said softly, 'We had some unholy rows, didn't we Rowan? Remember that?' he asked, pointing to the small scar on his cheek.

'Yes.' She remembered it very well. Moving to perch on the edge of the bed, tired of all the arguing, the tension, she clasped her knees to her chest and leaned back against the headboard. She'd hurled a dinner plate at him, and for once in her life her aim had been true. With an unconsciously mischievous grin, forgetting for a moment their differences, she pulled up the leg of her trousers to expose a scar on her shin. 'Remember this?'

'Yes. You fell over the groin at Portsmouth.'

'I did not fall!' she protested. 'You pushed me!'

Laughter softened his face, put a sparkle in his eyes as he leaned back against the window-sill. 'But not deliberately.'

'No, not deliberately.' Pulling down her trouser leg, she caught sight of her feet again. 'Look,' she murmured, extending one foot, half hoping, perhaps, that he would soothe her fears.

'Did you wear those boots on the flight?'

'Yes.'

'Then that's why. You should have worn comfortable old shoes. They'll be better by tomorrow.'

Her attention still on her feet, aware that he was still watching her, aware that something was different, she looked warily up.

'What a curious mixture you are,' he observed softly, and then smiled. 'My, but you were a handful.' As though the memory pleased him, his face softened yet further, and then he chuckled, 'Gazebo. You are a wretch, Rowan.'

'Did she ask?'

'Yes.'

'And did you tell her?'

'No.'

'I'm glad.'

'Because it was a private memory?'

'Yes,' she agreed softly as she fought not to be affected by the charm that he displayed so little. 'Although, according to you, it wasn't a gazebo but a Victorian summer house. Architecturally valuable.'

'I lied. It was definitely a gazebo; it said so in the real-estate blurb when I first viewed the place. "Sale of the contents of a desirable country residence",' he quoted, '"complete with gazebo". And you demolished it.'

'Unintentionally, and only because you provoked me!'

'It cost me a fortune!'

'You could afford it,' she grinned.

'Fortunately.'

'And you did make a good deal on the rest of the stuff.'

'True.'

'And it wasn't only me who had temper tantrums,' she continued quietly as she thought back. 'I seem to remember someone not a million miles away who threw my new set of golf clubs in the river.'

'Only because you tried to hit me with one of them— besides, you couldn't play for toffee.'

'Neither could you.'

'I can now.'

Because he had more time? Because he no longer had a wilful mistress to distract him? 'Can you?' she asked sadly.

'Yes.' With a laugh that sounded somehow hollow, he gave a rueful shake of his head. 'Violent pair, weren't we?'

'Yes,' she agreed.

'But not dull, Rowan. Never dull.'

'No. Frightening sometimes, exciting, like living on the edge of a volcano, but no, not dull.' Resting her chin on her drawn-up knees, her eyes on his strong face, she asked curiously, 'Do things seem dull for you now? Is that why Hetty said she was worried about you?'

'Dull? No, I don't have time for dullness.'

Like someone needing to probe an aching tooth, she asked, 'And Patricia? Is it serious?'

He shrugged, his face closed once more, and she wished that she hadn't asked. 'Although I'd have to be some sort of masochist, wouldn't I, to stick my head in the same noose twice? You'd think that being led by the nose by you would be more than enough.'

'Led by the nose?' she scoffed. 'Come on, Arden; that was one thing I never did. I'd like to have seen me try.'

'You didn't need to try; I was usually a very willing victim. And I swore I would never let you see how much you had hurt me, and yet here I am discussing it.'

Trying for indifference, she said glibly, 'Well, at least Patricia lives on the same side of the Atlantic.'

'Yes.'

'And hopefully only hurls insults,' she added naughtily.

He grinned, fingered his cheek. 'Yes, insults are— safer.'

'Would it have burned itself out, do you think? If I'd come with you? Or would we just have mellowed, the fire only smouldering?'

He grunted—amused or not she didn't know. 'Do you regret it, Rowan? The choice you made?'

Unable to gauge anything from his voice, she admitted quietly, 'I regretted there having to be one.'

'Still cautious, I see.'

With a small, meaningless smile that didn't touch her lovely eyes, she asked carefully, 'Do you?'

'Sometimes.' His gaze steady on hers, he added almost inaudibly, 'Come here.'

Immediately wary, on her guard, she asked, 'Why?'

'I don't ask twice, Rowan; you should know that. Either come or stay.'

'Then I'll stay,' she said, her throat dry. To do anything else would have been abominably stupid—even if he wasn't involved with Patricia. One touch from his strong hands and she'd give in; she knew she would. And there was to be no emotion; she'd *promised* herself that.

With an indifferent shrug, he began walking towards the door, and just when she thought she was safe, that the danger was past, he quickly turned and swept her backwards across the bed.

CHAPTER SIX

DON'T struggle, Rowan warned herself as Arden's hard body covered hers; to do so will only make him worse, make the torment greater. But it was unbelievably hard to remain still. Her breathing laboured, she said as quietly as she was able, 'Get off me, Arden.'

'And if I refuse?' he taunted.

Feeling almost ill, fighting to remain quiescent, she matched him stare for stare, then gave an unexpected jerk, which should have dislodged him and didn't. 'Worry over Hetty doesn't give you the right to use me,' she managed evenly.

'I'm not using you, and stop struggling; you'll only hurt yourself.'

'Then get off me.'

'Why did you come?'

'You know why I came; I thought Hetty was ill.'

'And you didn't think it odd that she wanted to meet you in my office in Boston?'

'Of course I thought it odd.' And disturbing, and frightening—and exciting, knowing that she would finally see him again. 'But I assumed there must be a reason.'

'Which there was.'

'Yes.'

'Beautiful Rowan,' he murmured, and the moment lengthened, became tense, stretched, became taut, and then her heart began to beat just a little bit faster. Her breath caught, remained suspended as he slowly lowered his mouth to hers. . .

'No!' Wrenching her face away, she stared determinedly at the wall.

'Just testing,' he drawled mockingly. Putting her aside as though she were of no more importance than an unwanted vase, he got easily to his feet, stood looking down at her. 'You want me, Rowan. I see it in your eyes, know it by the way you move. It churns in your insides, haunts your dreams—'

'No!'

'Yes.'

With an inarticulate sound in the back of her throat, she thrust herself upright, stared at him across the bed. Between them was a link that stretched to infinity. He knew. Conviction was written in his hard grey eyes. And he *knew* that she knew.

'All right,' she agreed harshly, 'you affect me. You could even make me respond. Is that what you want me to say? But whatever I might think, whatever I might feel I do not want you back in my life! I don't want to leave England! I don't want emotion! And I most certainly do not want this aggravation!'

'Don't you?' he taunted.

'No. Is it a game? Is that it? All right, I give in. You win. I concede. Happy now?'

'Ecstatic,' he drawled.

'I will not go through it all again,' she warned. *Couldn't!* It would destroy her.

'I'm not asking you to,' he said softly. 'Actually, I came to see if you wanted something to eat. The cooker's not yet connected. Pizza do you?' Without waiting for a reply he walked out—and left an echoing silence behind him.

Don't react, she told herself. Don't throw anything, just... Violently wrenching the duvet off the bed, she hurled it on the floor and stamped on it. I hate you, Arden. I hate you *so* much! Sinking down on the edge of the mattress, she put her head in her hands.

Why? She demanded of herself. Why do you continually lay yourself open to his taunts? Haven't you learned *anything* during this past year? Obviously not. And she couldn't hide in her room. Wouldn't give him the satisfaction of hiding in her room. But why had he behaved like that? Why? To pay her back? And he hadn't been unmoved, she thought drearily.

Deliberately keeping her mind away from the feel of him, the warmth, she found her socks, pulled them on and went downstairs, chin high—a wasted gesture because Arden was nowhere to be seen.

Going into the kitchen, she agitatedly began to rearrange the new canisters, stiffened when she heard his footsteps in the hall, kept her back to the door when she heard it open, and knew that he looked in. But thankfully, he didn't speak, and she let her breath out on a long, shaky sigh when she heard him go into his study. She felt as though she'd just run a long and very arduous race. How many days to fill in until Hetty came home?

And she'd told him the truth. She didn't want him. No, she mentally qualified, she didn't want to want him. Didn't want this aching pain inside, this yearning, because it was no more likely to work now than it had then.

Needing something constructive to do—something

to distract her—she began unpacking the boxes of kitchen equipment, utensils and china and finding homes for them in the new cupboards. She stacked the empty boxes out on the deck, picked up a cloth and began automatically wiping down surfaces.

She was beginning to feel displaced, alien. And, knowing that sitting and eating a pizza with him as though everything were normal would possibly be the straw that finally broke her, she made herself a sandwich with produce from the newly stocked fridge and went to bed before the pizza could be delivered.

The next day Arden was back to being terse. Whether it was her or some other cause, she didn't know, but, whatever the reason, things went from bad to worse. Tension built, became impossible to bear. Trying to avoid him became impossible to bear, and if she wasn't falling over workmen she was falling over boxes. Communication became an impossibility. She'd ask a question he'd give a terse, one-word answer, so Rowan gave up trying and just did what she thought best. You tried to help, tried to be pleasant and all you got for your pains was your nose snapped off.

So she kept her tongue between her teeth, her opinions to herself. It must have been some sort of a record, she decided gloomily, and even with Patricia, who made an art form of interfering, Rowan was remarkably restrained—but it wasn't easy and it took its toll. She began to think that if anyone so much as looked at her the wrong way she would explode.

She'd been in to Portland that morning, courtesy of one of the workmen who had had to go in for some supplies, and even though they'd only been gone a few hours that had been wrong. She'd received a look of disparagement for her low-heeled shoes and skirts, but she'd held her tongue and now he'd gone to visit Hetty and, for the moment at least, ther was peace.

But peace didn't seem to suit her either, and she was sick to death of the kitchen, she decided. Sick to death of trying to find more things to clean to keep herself occupied. Which didn't go unnoticed.

'Every time I see you you're cleaning those damned surfaces!' Arden castigated her as he strode through the backdoor. 'What are you trying to do? Get into the *Guinness Book of Records*?'

'Why not? I'm sure as hell not likely to get any records for putting up with you!' she retorted without thinking, then bit her lip, chagrined that he could so easily goad her. 'Sorry,' she muttered. 'I need to be occupied.'

'Then go and clear out the room I'm being forced to use, so that it can be decorated.'

'And I suppose that's my fault as well?'

'No,' he sighed. 'I have some work to do. If Tom wants me I'll be in the study.'

Nodding, she waited until he'd gone, then went up to inspect his room. She hadn't really noticed much about it when she'd come to call him when Hetty had been taken ill, but now saw that it held what was presumably the overflow from the other bedrooms. There was an old dressing table, two wardrobes, and, running along one wall, a high shelf that maybe once had held knick-knacks and now held a motley collection of rubbish.

A space had been cleared for his bed but that was about all. A door stood open in the corner, leading to

a bathroom. Returning downstairs, she collected an
empty cardboard box from the deck and then went
back to make a start. Half an hour later she heard him
come up, lean in the doorway.

'You don't have to do this.'

'Go away,' she ordered mildly, then held up the
strange-looking ornament that she'd taken from the
shelf, a query in her eyes.

'Pitch it. In fact, pitch everything except the bedding
and the few clothes I have up here.'

Nodding, she threw it into the box.

Moving into the room, he began to help her. 'You
should have changed into old clothes,' he murmured
as he too began to examine the articles on the shelf.

'I didn't bring any old clothes with me. I didn't know
I was going to be cleaning.'

'You don't need to now. I'm paying Mary Ann to do
so.' Picking up an old photo frame showing a faded,
grainy print of a young woman clearly from an earlier
era, he stared at it for some moments in silence. 'The
house belonged to an elderly gentleman,' he finally
explained. 'A nice old boy, but it was getting too much
for him and he moved up to Montreal to live with his
daughter.'

With a sigh, as though the memory made him sad,
he gently placed the photograph with the other stuff to
be thrown away. 'And one day, no doubt, someone
else will be doing the same for me. Speculating, maybe,
on what I was like.'

'They'd never come close,' she murmured sadly. If
she, who knew him now, didn't understand him, how
could anyone a hundred years hence? 'How was Hetty?'

'Fine. She's hoping to be discharged tomorrow.'

And, hard as it had been when he'd been terse, bad-tempered, this was worse, and she began to feel jangled again, tense, started to move away when he began feeling along with shelf towards where she stood.

Automatically beginning to turn when she heard his sudden curse, she felt something strike her on the back; wetness. . .

'What the. . .?' There was a sharp pain, a burning sensation. . . With a yell of alarm she swung round, trying to hold her sweater out from her skin. 'Whatever is it? What have you done?' Frantically trying to shrug out of her sweater, she yelled in fright, 'Get it off me!'

'I'm trying, dammit! Hold still!'

'I can't—Ow, Arden, it's burning!' Unable to keep still for the pain, she hopped around, with Arden trying to drag her sweater over her head and forcing her through the door into the bathroom and then under the shower.

Skidding on the wet tiles, she protested violently, 'For God's sake, Arden! I've still got my shoes on!'

'Then take them off!'

Muttering and whimpering, her voice muffled by the jumper still bundled round her neck, one arm in, one out, ice-cold water drenching her, she shivered convulsively and managed to kick off her shoes.

'Why the hell couldn't you wear a sweater with a decent opening?'

'Because I didn't know some idiot was going to drench me with acid!'

'It wasn't acid!'

'Then what the hell was it?'

'Some sort of cleaning fluid—I don't know—and keep still!' he shouted as he finally wrenched the sweater over her head, nearly taking her ears off in the process.

Frightened, bewildered by the speed of events, fumbling with the waistband of her skirt, clutching a soaked Arden as he helped her step out of it, she whispered, 'How bad is it?'

'I don't know; not bad, I think.' Unhooking the shower head, he sprayed the now warmer water down her back, thoroughly soaking it. 'The skin's not broken, just a bit red.'

'A bit?' she asked bitterly. 'I feel as though I've been in a fire.'

Turning off the water, he hung the head back up, turned her round and stared at her—at her sopping wet hair hanging in rats'-tails, her clinging, and very revealing, underwear—and murmured throatily, 'You *look* as though you've been in a fire.'

'But what on earth was it *doing* there? And haven't you got any towels in this place? I'm freezing!'

Grabbing a towel, he wrapped it round her and helped her into the bedroom. 'Solvent, I think.'

'Well, what the hell did someone want a solvent for? Unwelcome visitors?'

The laugh sounded dragged out of him, reluctant, and then he gave her a look of humorous exasperation. 'How the hell should I know? Perhaps it was used for ungluing stamps, pictures—or maybe not; perhaps the old boy *did* use it for unwelcome visitors.' Squelching back to the bathroom, he collected some cream from the medicine cabinet. 'Here, turn round; this should help.'

'What is it?' she asked suspiciously.

'Superglue, of course. I thought I might try sticking you to the bed. What the hell do you think it is?'

'Knowing you, probably arsenic!'

'Good guess, Rowan!' Wrenching the towel away, he thrust her face down on the bed. None too gently. 'Keep still; this might sting!'

'Oh, thanks a bunch! Ow—that's cold!'

'Don't be such a baby.' Spreading the antiseptic cream carefully across the red areas, unhooking her wet bra, he asked, 'How does that feel?'

'All right, I suppose,' she admitted grudgingly. 'Thanks.' Rolling over too soon, using her elbow to keep her back off the bed, she caught his arm, causing him to overbalance.

'For God's sake, Rowan, be careful! Now look what you've done!'

Squinting sideways, seeing the squashed tube, the worm of white goo spread on his duvet, she twisted aside, dislodging her bra, just as he reached out to pick up the tube—and his warm palm encountered a full, soft breast. Jerking back as though burned, they stared at each other in shock.

CHAPTER SEVEN

'OH, GOD,' Arden groaned, and whether he moved towards her or she towards him she didn't know; she knew only that their mouths met, clung, fused violently together. Months of denial went into that kiss. Months of wanting, needing. . . Of desire, aggravation, exasperation and pain. And these last few days of tension, of worry over Hetty, of being forced into proximity exploded into passion.

One large hand found that once familiar, special place—the warm gap between stocking-top and panties. His thumb began to rove along her groin; his other hand was used to facilitate his struggling out of his wet clothes, for removing entirely her sodden bra, and his mouth continued to ravage hers with savage intensity.

Their wet bodies soon grew warm, then hot, their breathing violent, laboured; his warm palm moved and she mumbled a protest as it smoothed up towards her full breasts, and she clung to him, sobbed in pleasure and in pain as he removed her pants, rolled to cover her—a warm, heavy weight, a weight too long denied.

His rhythmic thrusts were expected, familiar, as though it had only been yesterday that they had loved. There was pain because it had been a while since he had touched her, but it was a pain that she revelled in as they gave each other pleasure, gave in to overriding need. There was no consciousness, only desperation—

and fulfilment was swift, inevitable. As cries were torn from them, shredded by exploding breath, they slumped, clung, were silent.

'Don't say anything!' he insisted fiercely, his voice thick, as he held her impossibly tight, buried his face in her neck. 'Not one damn word!'

'No.'

'No analysis, no discussion, no what happens next!'

'No.'

'Don't move, don't talk; just stay quiet.'

Her eyes screwed tight, she forced her face further into the warmth of his shoulder, suspended thought, tried to stop feeling—and slowly tension eased, breathing became possible, and he lifted his head.

Staring down at her, his face still, without expression, he lowered his mouth to hers, began to kiss her almost gently, compulsively, and she relaxed into his embrace, urged the warmth of his flesh closer. They kissed like lovers, moved their bodies gently—an erotic dance in slow motion—and arousal was the most natural progression in the world.

This time it was languorous, exquisite torture, and still no words were said. Their bodies knew the rhythm now, remembered how it once had been, and fulfilment was a gentle climb, a sigh of thankfulness, incredible warmth and peace, and, perhaps because of the strain they'd both been under, they drifted into sleep.

One or the other of them must have surfaced briefly, because when Rowan woke the duvet was dragged across them, their bodies curved like spoons in a drawer. Opening her eyes, she stared blankly for a moment at iron-grey hair, at a tanned shoulder hunched above the covers, at the moon outside the window. . . Moon?

Reaching out carefully, she turned on the bedside light and then gave a convulsive shiver. Her knees were thrust up beneath warm buttocks, both arms had encircled a strong body, one hand still lay flat against his chest, the arm trapped beneath him. Her mouth had been pressed to his warm back and she felt desire spiral through her.

She wanted so very much to press herself closer, instigate his arousal. Wanted him to turn to her, smile, beg her to stay. Would he? Was that really what she wanted? Yes, it was, and she didn't want to move, wanted this moment to go on for ever. She felt as though she had finally come home.

Unconsciously, or perhaps consciously, she began to move her fingers on his warm skin, rested her cheek against his warm back—and felt him stiffen. She held her breath, wondered, wished desperately that she knew what he was thinking. Unable to see his face, she could only speculate, pray.

He gave a little grunt—of anger? Disgust?—and then he was moving, thrusting the cover aside, swinging his long legs over the edge of the bed. He turned, gave her one long, comprehensive look, shuddered like a man just emerging from a nightmare, and walked away. Unhooking his robe from the back of the door, he hesitated, then threw it at her without looking. Then he picked up the wet towel from the floor, knotting it round his hips, and walked out.

Staring at the closed door and then down at herself, she saw that she was still wearing her suspender belt and stockings. They looked incredibly stupid. Feeling

totally uncoordinated, shaken, she stared at her watch.
Half past eight. They'd slept for over three hours.

And what happens now? she wondered. Nothing?
He was just going to walk out, say nothing, ignore it?
Searching her mind for regret, disgust, she found none,
only a sadness for what she had once thrown away.
And a need for more.

Feeling extraordinarily reluctant, she got up, winced,
and remembered her back. The skin felt a bit tight, a
bit sore, but nothing too bad. Twisting sideways, she
tried to see it in the mirror. A faint red weal—that was
all there was to see—a faint red weal that had caused
so much drama.

Angrily ripping off the offending suspender belt and
stockings, she walked into the bathroom. Like a sleep-
walker she washed, used his comb to untangle her hair,
used his toothbrush to clean her teeth, stared without
seeing at her discarded clothing. Wrapping herself in
his robe, she went downstairs.

He'd made a pot of coffee and was sitting at the
kitchen table, a mug nursed in his palms. Without
speaking, afraid for once of saying the wrong thing,
she filled a mug for herself and joined him. But when
the silence went on too long, when her nerves could
take no more, she asked huskily, 'What happens now?'

'Nothing happens now,' he said flatly.

'Don't be silly; we—'

'Silly?' he roared, making her jump. '*Silly?*'

'Yes, we had—did. . .' Inarticulate for the first time
in her life, as far as she could remember, she took a
determined breath and blurted out, 'We made love;
you can't just ig—'

'We had sex!' he bit out helpfully. 'Men and women do it all the time.'

'I don't,' she argued stupidly.

'Go away!' he thundered. Slamming down his mug, he got up and stormed out.

Oh, God. With a long shudder, she slid her hands roughly over her hair. What to do now? Nothing? Just get up, get dressed? Pretend it never happened? Pretend he meant nothing to her? Pretend she could live the rest of her life without him?

This last year she'd pretended—pretended she was over him, shoved the memories aside, ruthlessly suppressed her feelings—and what had it got her? A health club that was now bigger than she'd intended, bordering on the impersonal—the very thing she hadn't ever wanted—a lot of sleepless nights, a workload that was exhausting. . .

Picking up her mug, she took a sip of coffee. All you ever wanted, Rowan, was to be an aromatherapist, she reminded herself. A self-employed aromatherapist. You didn't want an empire, paperwork, accounts. . .

Her sigh deep, she examined what she should have examined a long, long time ago. Her parents' obstructive behaviour had pushed her into a determination to be independent, only ever answering to herself. And then Arden—Arden's own arrogance—had pushed her into biting off more than she could chew. More than she wanted to chew. But, having said she wanted an empire, an empire was what she'd built.

But she had never expected that it would take off as it had. She'd expected to struggle, fight to make ends meet, but, as though the gods were mocking her, it had all come so unbelievably easily. The right place at the right time. And she wanted to go back to what she had only ever wanted in the first place—a small salon that provided aromatherapy and reflexology, with maybe one other girl to assist. Not a health club, not a staff of ten.

She'd had a plan, a dream, and because people had scoffed, said she would never do it—not in a recession; she was too young, too inexperienced—she had made the dream bigger. And won—because of her determination to be taken seriously. And now there was jealousy and take-over bids—and she wanted to cry. Did she really only want it so that she could boast that she had it? And who, apart from herself, actually cared? No one.

And she loved him. Had always loved him. Since the day he'd appeared on her doorstep she'd loved him. She had opened the door to him—and then just stared. As had he. Unbelievable that both had felt the same.

When opportunity came knocking you either ignored it or grabbed it with both hands and damned the consequences. Rowan had grabbed it because the creature of impulse that she had been meant to be briefly surfaced, because Arden had that effect on women, made them think that the moon was in reach— and she had then spent the next few months torn betwen practicality and emotion. That was partly why their relationship had been so stormy—because her mind had been at war with her body.

And now? Now she didn't think that she could bear to go through another year of regret, of wanting, of feeling only half-alive. And after their lovemaking— not sex, she told herself—the way he'd responded. . . Which must mean, mustn't it, that he felt the same?

Ever since she'd arrived she'd been fighting him, fighting her feelings because he'd said that he didn't care, but now... So if you have to eat crow, Rowan, then eat it, and pretend you enjoy the taste, because he *is* worth fighting for. He is what you want.

Glancing up at the ceiling, as though she might be able to see him above, feeling nervous and uncertain, she made her decision. And if he didn't want her?

With a determined little breath, she put down her mug, pushed back her chair and went to find him. Hurrying upstairs, she caught her foot in the hem of his dressing gown, stumbled, grabbed frantically at the newel post—and saw him standing at the end of the shadowy landing, fully dressed.

'Arden?' she called quietly. 'Can we talk?'

'About what?' he asked unhelpfully, and his voice was flat, cold, hollow.

'Us.'

'There is no us,' he denied brutally.

'Yes, there is. After—'

'After what? Sex?'

'It wasn't sex,' she insisted desperately. 'It was—more. And you can't pretend it didn't happen!'

Striding towards her, he grasped her chin, held her face up to his, his gaze merciless. '*Nothing* happened. Nothing that doesn't happen every minute of every day all over the world. You nearly destroyed me once, do you know that?'

'No,' she whispered huskily.

'No, like you don't know anything else in your busy little life that doesn't concern the pursuit of wealth!'

'That isn't fair,' she protested. 'You know it isn't. It wasn't like that.'

'Wasn't it?' he asked bleakly.

'No. I'll give it up,' she promised recklessly. 'The club, everything. . .'

'I don't want you to give it up. I don't want anything you have to give.,'

'But it can't *end*! Not like this, not after. . .' Eyes pleading, one hand on his arm, not believing that he meant what he was saying, she tried to smile, and he disdainfully removed her hand from his arm.

'It ended a long time ago,' he stated flatly, and yet, for a moment, he had sounded almost on the edge of desperation himself. But not now. 'Go back to your shelving experts, your young, upwardly mobile lovers.'

'I don't *have* any lovers!'

'No?' he sneered.

'No! My God, you make me sound like a. . . And don't you ever listen to *anything* I say?'

'Listen to what? Every damned time I came over you had a different man in tow!'

'I've never had anyone in tow! And *when* did you come over? I haven't seen you since—'

'You gave me my marching orders,' he finished distastefully.

Staring at him, angry and disbelieving, trying frantically to recall *any* man she'd had in tow, she frowned. 'You've been watching me?'

'No, I *saw* you. A subtle difference.'

'When?'

'Does it matter?'

'Yes.' But there hadn't been any. . . 'Do you mean Donald?'

'Donald? Who the hell is Donald?'

'Fair hair, slim. . .'

'I didn't take *details*, Rowan! And this argument is unutterably pointless.'

'Not to me it isn't.' Staring up at him, into hard grey eyes, she asked quietly, 'You came to see me? After. . . Did you?'

'Maybe.'

'Why? Please, Arden, tell me why.'

'Because I thought the club would fail,' he said derisively. 'Thought you might need the pieces picked up. Thought you might—relent. What did you know about business management? Running a gym? Nothing! Only every time I saw you. . .'

'Every time?' she whispered.

'It was a little bit bigger, a little bit better,' he continued with savage intensity, as though she hadn't spoken. 'An extension here, an extension there—and you were doing very nicely, thank you. You didn't need me! And I felt crucified.'

Her eyes wide, aching with the weight of unshed tears, she just continued to stare at him. 'I didn't know,' she whispered. 'I thought. . .' Thought that he had accepted her dismissal and never thought about her again. Which was why. . . 'I didn't know,' she repeated. 'How could I know? You were so scathing when we parted, and you certainly never gave the impression of a man wanting me back.'

'You think you're the only one with pride?'

This was the same man who arrogantly overrode everyone's feelings? Who'd started a string of businesses from nothing? Who forcefully went after everything he ever wanted? 'Did Hetty know?'

'Of course not! You think I advertised my folly?'

'Folly?' Staring up at him, running his words over in

her mind, she shook her head. 'No,' she said quietly, 'I don't believe you. If you had really wanted me, an army of men wouldn't have stopped you.'

'Wouldn't they?'

'You expect me to believe that we drifted further and further apart because, against all the odds, I made a success of my little enterprise?'

'No. Because you'd shown very clearly that you didn't need me.'

'But I did!' she exclaimed on a hollow laugh. 'And if you'd crooked your little finger—just once—I'd have abandoned it all.'

'Would you?' he asked sceptically.

'Yes.'

'Then what a pity neither of us ever bothered to crook fingers!'

Staring at him, at this hard man who hadn't, as she'd thought, left her never to return, she swallowed drily and said thickly, 'Will you crook your finger now?' And he laughed.

'Now? Oh, no, Rowan. Now is far too late.'

Her lovely eyes full of pain, she whispered, 'Is it?'

'Yes.'

'Why?'

'Because I no longer want you. I suggest you go and get dressed. Or go to bed. Abandon hope, Rowan,' he added cruelly. 'I have other fish to fry.'

'Like Patricia?'

He didn't answer, just continued to stand there, watching her, and she couldn't let it go, not like this. Couldn't let it *end*. 'If you'd tried to persuade me. . .' she began.

'Persaude? Oh, no, lady, I don't persuade anyone.

You either loved me or you didn't; persuading didn't come into it.'

'Of course it did! I couldn't just uproot myself!'

'Why not?'

'Because I had responsibilities!'

'Like a new lease,' he agreed. 'Pick me up, put me down. . .'

'What?'

'You! As though I were one of your damned stuffed toys!'

'No!'

'Yes!' he hissed. 'You didn't expect me to fly over at the drop of a hat when you had time for me? Fly back when you didn't? Well, I don't wish to conduct a love affair long distance. Go back to your empire, Rowan, and leave me in peace.'

'I won't beg again,' she warned.

'Good.'

'If I go, I won't come back. Ever.'

'Good. Phone's ringing.' Pushing past her, he thundered down the stairs and into his study.

With a little shudder, she stared at nothing. He really didn't want her. Their lovemaking had meant nothing. Unclamping her hands from the newel post, she walked somewhat dazedly into her room. *Really* didn't want her?

In the distant recesses of her mind she heard the front door open and close, saw the faint glow as the porch light came on, and she walked to the window, stared out, saw Arden stride down the path, saw him hesitate, halt—and then saw Patricia hurry towards him. She was holding a sheaf of papers and she looked happy, excited, saying words that Rowan couldn't hear,

and then she flung her arms round his neck—and they
kissed.

Wrenching her eyes away, an unconscious gasp of
pain escaping her, Rowan clenched her hands tight in
the curtain. She had thought. . . Oh, dear God, she had
thought that it would be all right. Had thought, hoped,
expected that when she came out to the States it would
be all right. Despite the arguments, the sniping, her
own determination, a part of her—a very large part of
her, she finally admitted—had thought that they'd be
able to work it out. Had thought that he must still feel
as she did. Despite her denials, she hadn't thought that
it would end like this.

Disbelief still lingering in her eyes, she stayed where
she was for long, long moments, absently registered
the rising wind, a distant rumble of thunder, and then,
her sigh long, shuddery, despairing, without looking
again at the two figures on the front lawn, she quietly
drew the curtains.

The ache inside too big to contain, feeling almost ill,
she crumpled down beside the bed and began to cry.
Screwing the duvet up against her face, she gave in to
her misery. Cried for all the might-have-beens. Cried
because there was no one on this earth who understood
her, knew her for the person she was.

Don't Rowan; ah, don't; come on, don't let him win;
don't let it hurt so; don't cry; please don't cry. You
said no emotion. You *said* that! Gritting her teeth,
holding her breath, she fought to compose herself.
Breathing deeply, she rested her cheek against the soft
bedding, staring bleakly at nothing.

Nobody loved her—not one single, solitary person.
She was nobody's child, because her parents could not

forgive her for 'abandoning' them, as they put it; nobody's lover, because she had not known that he'd come back and now it was too late. She had one or two friends who were, presumably, fond of her—but if she died tomorrow there would be no one whose heart would ache because she was no longer there...

But crucified? As she had been? Pride and determination and hurt—and now he was Patricia's.

Gathering the rags of that same pride about her now, she got to her feet. She had a skill, money in her account, somewhere to live—and none of it at the moment seemed to mean a damn thing, because without Arden in it the future looked bleak and empty.

And he hadn't even cared enough to listen to her. Well, she wouldn't beg any more. She would go away, try to forget him... Or book into a hotel for the night, go and see Hetty in the morning, and then leave. Because she could not stay.

Wiping away tears that continued to fall, swallowing sobs that threatened to split her chest apart, she began to pack. It was over. Finally, it was over. No more hopes about him, no more dreams; she would throw herself into her work—make her empire even bigger?—and remain an independent lady. A maiden lady, like Hetty. Growing ever more tart? Brittle? Perhaps she should get a dog, a parrot...

Holding the breath in her throat, shutting her eyes tight for a moment, she fought down the tears and left. Had he still been in the front yard she would have walked past him, but he wasn't. And she didn't look back.

It was only a mile to the village but the wind seemed stronger; it hurled the rain against her in spiteful gusts, plastered leaves against her coat, seemed to be trying to push her backwards, back towards the house. She had arrived in a storm and was leaving in one. Someone must be trying to tell her something.

Entering the outskirts of the small community, her case banging uncomfortably against her leg, she walked past the little post office, the craft shop... There was no one about... Well, of course there was no one about, she told herself impatiently; anyone with any sense was safely indoors!

The capricious wind seemed to be plucking leaves from raked lawns and then hurling them around in a crazy dance, as though determined to punish those who were tidy. A piece of newspaper, plucked from someone's hand, perhaps, was plastered like some bizarre poster against the route-marker, and she just wanted to huddle somewhere warm and go to sleep, forget that Arden had ever existed. Ease the pain inside.

Hair whipped all over her face by the gusting wind, she fought her way towards the hotel, then staggered inside. It was a haven of blissful peace. Dropping her suitcase in front of the desk, she leaned on the comforting, stable wood for a moment to get her breath back. Determined not to give in to her pain, she rang the little brass bell. It gave a soft, unimportant ping.

A door opened in the rear and a middle-aged lady bustled out. She had dark hair going grey, warm brown eyes and a friendly smile. 'Yes? Oh, my goodness, what on earth happened to you? No, don't tell me,' she added humorously. 'You've obviously been out in this wretched gale. You came by car? Not the best weather for touring. You need a room?'

'Yes, please, just for the night, 'I—'

'My goodness,' the woman giggled, 'we seem to have been invaded by the Brits. Sorry,' she apologised, handing the resiter to Rowan to sign. 'It's just that someone said Arden had an English lady staying up at the h— Oh.' Her eyes fixed on Rowan's signature.

'Yes.'

'Rowan, is it? I know the name was something to do with a tree... Sorry.' She grimaced. 'I didn't mean to be rude. How's Hetty?' she went on hastily.

'Oh, fine; she's being released tomorrow.'

'Tomorrow?' she queried. 'Then why. . .?' Taking in Rowan's case, then Rowan, her brown eyes begged a question, but she didn't ask, so Rowan didn't volunteer why she was looking for a room in a hotel the day before her godmother was sent home. 'None of my business, is it?' She grinned.

'Name's Betty Logan,' she finally introduced herself, 'and now is not the time for lengthy explanations. You're tired—and hurt,' she added with a gentle smile, and at the first kind word in what seemed like such a long time Rowan felt her eyes fill with fresh tears. 'So before we do anything else we'd best have a look at that cut!'

'Cut?'

'On your forehead.'

Putting up a shady hand, Rowan touched her fingers above her right eye; they came away sticky with blood. She didn't remember getting cut. A twig or something must have caught her. Not that it mattered.

With an indifferent glance at her reflection in the mirror behind the desk, she saw that her hair was a tangled mess, lavishly decorated with twigs and leaves;

blood was smeared across one cheek, dirt on the other, and the deep scratch above her right eyebrow was still sluggishly bleeding. Delightful, Rowan, she thought. Entirely delightful. And her green eyes looked—dead

Automatically brushing debris from her hair, she murmured unconcernedly, 'I don't think it's deep. I'll deal with it later.'

'All right,' Betty agreed dubiously, 'but if you take my advice you'll have a nice hot bath and then get into bed. Room three's free.'

Taking a key from the row of hooks behind her, she lifted the flap in the counter, then stopped as the street door was flung open. 'Someone else caught out in the storm. . .' she began, and then halted as Arden strode in. She glanced from one to the other, took in Rowan's tight, mutinous expression, Arden's empty one, and slowly lowered the flap.

'Are you entirely out of your mind?' he demanded scathingly.' Just look at you! It's blowing a gale out there! You could have been killed!'

'Yeah, and wouldn't that have solved a few problems?' Rowan spat back.

'Oh, don't be so stupid!'

'And don't you pretend you bloody care!' she retorted furiously. 'But don't you worry; just as soon as this storm blows itself out, I shall be out of your hair for good!'

'Well, what the hell did you expect? Approbation? You never even mentioned his name!'

'*Whose* name?'

'Donald's!' he spat.

Confused, weary, hurting so *much*, she demanded,

'Why should I? He wasn't any of your damned business!'

'Thanks!' he bit out savagely. 'So where is he now?'

'Timbuktu,' she snapped. 'We have an assignation there in order to screw up someone else's life!' Swinging round to the riveted Betty, she demanded, 'Key?'

But before the woman could meekly hand it over— all the lights went out.

CHAPTER EIGHT

'OH, NOW what?' Rowan heard Arden exclaim wearily.

'Perhaps it's only a blown fuse,' she said stupidly as she tried to accustom her eyes to the dark.

'Doubtful. On this day of disasters nothing could be that simple.'

She heard him move, heard his mumbled curse as he walked into something, followed by the opening of a door.

Never one to stay put and wait on events, and not wanting to be left on her own in the dark, hands held out in front of her, she groped for the desk. She could hear other doors opening, hesitant voices, and as she stumbled jarringly against her suitcase a wavering torch beam sprang to life.

'I've got some candles here somewhere,' Betty claimed as she handed the torch to Arden and began to search under the desk. 'Anyone got any matches or a lighter?' There was the sound of further rummaging, a curse, then a triumphant cry. 'Never mind, I've found some. Arden? Are you there?'

'Where else would I be?' he asked tiredly as he swung the torch onto her face.

Yes, where else would he be? Rowan wondered drearily. And yet, in an emergency, Arden was definitely the one to be beside. He probably *always* knew what to do. No doubt Betty would be eternally grateful.

'Where did Rowan get to?' Betty asked as she fumbled to light the candles.

'I didn't get to anywhere,' Rowan answered, wondering how much longer this nightmare was going to go on, and as the candle-flame flickered and flared she made her way across to one of the chairs that dotted the reception area.

Why was he here? she wondered as she collapsed into the chair. But it didn't even really seem to matter any more. Perhaps she'd been overloaded with too much drama in one day; whatever the reason, she suddenly felt too tired to make any more decisions. Shrugging out of her coat, kicking off her boots, she leaned back and closed her eyes. Life would go on very well without her.

There were sundry thumps, rustlings, slow movements, and she wearily opened her eyes. In the wavering light of the candles she watched other guests begin to filter down, watched Arden as he capably fixed several more candles round the room. He looked tired, tough, arrogant and capable. Had he followed her here? Or had he been coming to the village anyway? No way of knowing without asking—and she wasn't going to do that.

People began to sit in the other chairs, like at a party, expectant, eager. There were some who complained—inevitable, she supposed—as though an electricity failure had been sent expressly to thwart them or was somehow the fault of the hotel. There was humour, speculation, and one—there was always one, wasn't there?—who simply had to state the obvious. 'Tree brought down a power line, I guess.'

'Yes,' someone else agreed drily.

Arden's approach was soft, noiseless, his image barely discernible, and she turned her face away. She didn't want to look at him, remember how it had been—how *he* had been—just a short while ago.,

'All right?' he asked, and his voice was distant, controlled.

'I'm fine,' she said shortly. What else could she say? Inside I'm dying?

'We have to talk,' he continued, still brusque.

'No, we don't,' he retorted fiercely. 'It's too late for talking! You said so.' And then, unable to help herself, she turned her head towards him. 'Twice you've done this to me!' she hissed. 'Refused to listen! Made up your own mind! Well, you don't get a chance of a third—'

'I'm listening now,' he interrupted.

'Now is too late. And you aren't listening with any degree of understanding, only judgement, because you don't believe that I have anything to say that will make any difference.'

'You don't know that.'

'Yes, I do; I can see by your face. Go away, Arden; get out of my life!'

Bending forward, one hand on either side of her chair, he said with quiet savagery, 'This has got to go down in history as the most god-awful week anyone has ever spent! Not only have I had to contend with trying to get the house straight, I have had Hetty to worry about, a red-headed ex-mistress whose eyes spit sparks and tongue drips venom, and a rival whose dirty-tricks campaign almost brought my businesses to their knees!

'You aggravate me, arouse me, and then, standing there in a dressing gown several sizes too large, showing every part of you that constantly drives me insane, you expect me to hold a rational discussion on whether we should get back together! So *who* is Donald?'

'My manager,' she snapped.

'And the ape with muscles on his kneecaps?'

'I don't know any ape. . .' The warning glitter in his eyes prompted her into honesty. 'The club's fitness instructor!'

'Neither of whom you are having an affair with?'

'No.'

'Good.'

'Not good,' she retorted with just as much savagery, 'because now is too *late*; you said so!'

'So I did,' he sighed wearily.

'*And* you were kissing her!'

'Who?'

'Patricia!'

'Correction: *she* was kissing *me*!'

'Why?'

'Because she felt like it! Oh, damn you, Rowan!' he exclaimed tiredly. 'Damn you, damn you, damn you. I—' Only, before he could say whatever it was he'd been going to say, explosion split the night apart—burst onto their dulled senses like Armageddon.

'Oh, dear God,' Rowan whispered as she jerked upright. 'What the hell was that?' But Arden had already gone. She saw his shadowy leap as he ran to the front doors, saw the red glow of flames beyond them, heard the terrifying roar, the crackle and spit of burning.

Galvanised into action, she began to hurry after him. Everyone else was beginning to crowd in the doorway to watch and Rowan had to squirm her way between them. The bright glow clearly highlighted Arden as he dashed across the road, followed more slowly by two other men. She saw him halt, grab a woman who was shouting... Rowan knew that she was shouting even though she could hear nothing above the crackle of the fire that seemed to be rapidly consuming the wood-frame house at the end of the row opposite, knew that she was hysterical, and a cold hand clasped her insides—a dread knowledge.

Betty was standing beside her, she discovered, and she grasped her arm. 'Who...?'

'She has a babe...' Betty began, and then was unable to continue.

'Oh, dear G—!' And Rowan knew, even before she'd finished the exclamation, what would happen next. 'No!' she shouted as she shoved her way ruthlessly through the press of people. 'Arden, no!'

She had no boots on, no coat, and gave no thought to either as she broke into a run, tried desperately to reach him before he disappeared into the inferno. She gave no thought to what had happened between them, only knew that she had to stop him.

The wind was driving the fire into a frenzy, throwing heat across the road, maliciously buffeting her, making progress difficult. 'Oh, Arden, no,' she whispered helplessly. Someone grabbed her, made her stop, and she turned on them in fury.' Let me go!'

'No,' he urged thickly. 'It's hopeless. Look at it.'

She didn't want to look at it. She knew what she would see, and what she didn't see her imagination would conjure up. But she had to do something. She couldn't just stand here and watch him die.

Everyone else had joined them now. The whole village possibly. So many people. Someone with a brain had found their garden hose, was trying, trying... And it was too little. Someone else the the same... And still Arden didn't come out.

The mother of the baby was kneeling, screaming, being held by another woman—and Rowan suddenly had the feeling that Arden would come out the back. A *knowledge*, a desperate hope...

Breaking free from the man who still held her, she made a wide, dashing detour round the burning house, dodged flying debris, burning wood, knew someone was chasing after her, didn't stop, couldn't stop, scrambled over the fence into the back yard—just as a rear-bedroom window shattered with an explosive crack and they all froze in shock.

It seemed to happen almost in slow motion. The shower of glass, the flames, smoke, the dark figure clutching what looked like bedclothes, his slow leap, the thud as he hit the ground...and then time speeded up again, and she was running towards the still figure lying on his back. Someone grasped the bundle and a baby screamed. Part of her mind registered it, absorbed it, was glad, but the rest of her was concentrated on Arden, who lay so very still. A sob caught in her throat and she thumped her fist impotently on his chest.

'Don't you die!' she shouted fiercely. 'Don't you *dare* bloody die!'

There was a long exhalation of breath, a groan, and he opened his eyes, blinked. Rolling onto his side, he began to cough, then retch.

On her knees, her arms protectively round him, tears running down her cheeks, she gave a choked laugh that owed more to hysteria than humour, then cried, sniffed. 'You fool, you fool; how could you do something like that? How could you be so stupid? You might have been killed!'

Still coughing, still trying to get a decent breath into his lungs, he flopped over onto his back, arms spread wide, and just looked up at her.

Furious, exasperated, frightened, she slowly released him, sat back on her heels. 'I thought you were dead,' she whispered.

'So did I,' he confessed sombrely, his voice still cracked, husky. 'So did I.' They both looked towards the fire and in their shared look was the knowledge that things would never be quite the same again. 'Lucky to only break both legs.'

'What?' Staring down at him, she whispered huskily, 'Oh, Arden, no. Are they? Truly?'

With a muffled grunt, which might have been a cough or might have been laughter, he shook his head. 'I don't know.'

'And we can't call an ambulance or the fire brigade because the phones are out...' she began worriedly.

'But we do have a resident doctor,' an amused voice said from behind her. 'And if you two have finished this lengthy but hardly private conversation I would like to examine my patient. Move over, young lady; you're blocking the light.'

Shuffling to one side so that the glow from the fire

could highlight Arden's body, Rowan relinquished her place to the doctor. He nudged her and she hastily dragged her wandering mind back to the present.

'Pay attention. Hold my bag, there's a good girl.'

Automatically taking it, she watched as he swiftly checked Arden's pulse.

'Not the best place to carry out an examination, my boy, but needs must when the devil drives.' Wrenching up Arden's sweater, he put his stethoscope to his chest, listened, grinned and removed it. 'I don't think you're about to meet your maker just yet. Let's have a look at those legs.'

'How's the baby?' Arden croaked.

'By some miracle none the worse. However, I got Pat Reed to drive baby and mum to the hospital, just to be on the safe side. Smoke inhalation doesn't do a lot for little lungs. Well,' he finally pronounced as he ran his hands gently up and down Arden's legs, 'can't find any obvious breaks, but, like the little one, best to be safe than sorry; won't hurt to get some X-rays done.'

'Tomorrow.'

'Tonight.'

'Tomorrow,' Arden insisted, pushing himself into a sitting position and experimentally moving his legs. 'Thank God for soft ground to land on.'

'Amen to that,' the doctor agreed. Turning his attention to the still burning house, he continued sombrely, 'Not much to thank God about in that, is there? Although they seem to be managing to stop it from spreading to the next house. For now. Let's hope the wind doesn't chan— Do you get the feeling it's dropping?' he suddenly asked, and everyone in the

little group round them cocked their heads as though
listening.

'Perhaps the damn thing's blown itself out. Come
on, let's see if you can walk. Well, don't just stand
there like a loon, Bob Larkin! Take his other arm!'

Bob, with a sheepish grin, hurried to do his bidding,
and between them they helped Arden to his feet. He
stood gingerly for a moment, testing his weight, then
indicated for them to release him. Catching sight of
Rowan still kneeling in the mud, he said soberly and
yet somehow teasingly, 'I'm past praying for, Rowan;
might as well get up.'

The general laugh released tension, set the world
back on an even keel—or everybody else's world,
thought Rowan—and she gratefully accepted someone's hand to help her up. Staring at the burning
house, she shuddered, and violently forced away a very
vivid image of Arden burning to death. Forced away
the knowledge that she was now redundant, and that
she felt like a fool. 'What caused it? Does anyone
know?' she blurted out huskily.

'She was heating the baby's feed when the electricity
went,' the doctor explained, 'and like an idiot, like
most of us when we want to do something, she had the
bright idea of trying to light the old camping stove that
had been abandoned in the garage attached to the side
of the house.

'Well, she lit it all right—damn thing went up like a
flare—so she rushed into the kitchen to get some
water—and whilst she was gone the fire obviously
spread to whatever else was stored in the garage,
because the next thing she knew—wham! The whole
place went up like the fourth of July. She was blown

off her feet—blown right through the back door in fact, and then couldn't get back in for the flames. She ran round to the front, saw that was alight too, saw our hero. . .'

'Hmm,' Arden grunted. Grabbing Rowan's arm, he muttered, 'Time to go.'

He was embarrassed, she thought in surprise. She didn't know why she was surprised, but she was, and she couldn't shrug away with everyone watching, could she? Couldn't make him look foolish. . . With a shaky sigh, she reluctantly slid her arm round his waist and began to help him from the garden. He was trying very hard not to limp. Biting her lip, she wondered if she ought to insist that someone take him to be X-rayed.

As though reading her thoughts, as though he knew her too well, he said softly, 'No. I'm all right.'

With a resigned nod, she smiled vaguely at those still standing around and helped Arden over the low fence. There was nothing more they could do. The rest of the men in the village would, presumably, continue to fight the fire, and no doubt the man who had run the woman and her baby to the hospital would alert the fire services. And the wind *was* dropping, she thought as she helped Arden across the road. It was definitely calmer.

Betty fell into step beside them and they all trudged tiredly into the hotel. Taking charge, Betty pointed to two comfy armchairs. 'Sit,' she commanded. 'And whilst you two were playing Modesty Blaise and Batman we, the ladies of the village and myself, have been making coffee and sandwiches. We managed to unearth a couple of camping stoves, so before you do anything else you sit and have something to eat and drink. After that, well. . .' With a wide grin, she walked away, to return seconds later with a plate of sandwiches and two cups of coffee.

Arden eyed the coffee, gave her an old-fashioned look and waited. Betty grinned and went to unearth a bottle of bourbon. 'Better?'

'Much. Thanks.'

'I suppose you deserve it.' Looking down at him for a moment, she added softly, 'You could have been killed.'

'I know,' he agreed. 'I have the bruise to prove it.' Glancing at Rowan, he rubbed his chest where she had thumped him and she quickly looked away. Had there been a message in that glance? She didn't know; she just wanted to go away, be by herself.

'You're a damn fool,' Betty continued reprovingly to Arden, 'but thank the good Lord for it. Houses can be replaced.'

'Yes. If they need somewhere to stay, I have room up at my house. A bit basic,' he added ruefully, 'but adequate.' As he had once said to Rowan. 'What about her husband?'

'They'll alert the police from the hospital, ask them to find him. His firm will have his schedule—he's a rep,' she explained. 'Now, eat up. I've instructed everyone not to use the hot water, so there should be enough left in the tank for you both to have a bath. I'll take some candles up to your room—and see to that cut, Rowan,' she insisted, sounding almost fierce.

Surprised, Rowan touched her fingers to her forehead and encountered a nasty, sticky mess. Perhaps she'd knocked it again. She didn't remember doing so but with everything else that had been going on that was hardly surprising.

'Maybe you're the one who should be going to the hospital,' he said softly. Turning her head towards him in order to examine the cut, he took in her pinched white face, and sighed. 'Are you all right?'

'Yes,' she whispered, and knew that she wasn't. And at that moment it felt as though nothing would be all right ever again. Trying so very hard to cope with the overwhelming feeling of desolation that washed over her, she took a sandwich that she didn't want—then put it back.'I think I'll go on up,' she added shakily.

Shivering with reaction, she got to her feet, and only then realised how wet and cold they were. Glancing down, she stared at her mud-caked socks, the soaked knees of her jeans. Arden followed her glance and smiled tiredly.

'Have to do it different, don't you?'

'Yes.' And then Tom thrust through the outer door, closely followed by Patricia. He glanced quickly round, spotted Arden, and hurried across. 'You OK? Someone just said you'd been in the fire.'

'I'm fine.'

'Anyone hurt?'

'No.'

'Thank God. Hi, Rowan,' he added, and she managed a faint smile, the merest movement of her lips, but he didn't seem to notice as he turned back to Arden and grinned. 'We've got him!' he exclaimed gleefully. 'This time I think we've got him!'

Patricia put a hand on Arden's shoulder, smiled at him, and Rowan hurriedly grabbed up her coat and boots. She couldn't stay, couldn't watch and listen. . .

Hurrying away, she heard Patricia's soft voice exclaiming and she shut her ears and her mind. Room three, Betty had said what seemed like a lifetime ago, and she prayed that the key would be in the door. She'd had more than enough for one day—more than enough for one lifetime, and making polite conversation with Patricia and her uncle would be just too damned much.

Once in the sanctuary of her room she stared blindly at the pink candles. One on each bedside table. Like an altar. Tears of tiredness and despair running down her face, she collapsed onto the side of the bed. She wanted to leave. Now. Run away. Only, at the moment, there was nothing to leave in—and it felt as though there was nowhere far enough away to hide.

A candle had been placed in the bathroom, she saw; it flickered eerily through the half-open door, made giant shadows on the wall. A red glow still lit the window, three scarlet stripes across the bed—the bed that she yearned to climb into, close her eyes.

The door opened and she jerked round defensively as Arden walked in.

'God, I ache,' he declared as he slumped tiredly onto the bed beside her.

Staring at him, she gave him an ineffectual push. 'Go away, Arden!' she exclaimed despairingly. 'Go home.' When he didn't move, she jumped to her feet and hurried to the bathroom. 'I have to have my bath.'

'Rowan?'

She almost got the door closed but not quite, and she stared at him defiantly through the crack that he was keeping open with his foot, and only then did she take in how exhausted he looked. Gazed helplessly at his dirty, soot-smeared face.

His eyelashes were a bit singed, she saw. One eyebrow scorched and comical. The ends of his grey hair were burnt, looked as though they would be brittle to the touch. His sweater had a couple of burn holes and his hands, resting on the doorframe, were mottled with nasty red and black patches.

'A bit battered,' he commented softly. 'Don't want me any more, Rowan?'

With a broken little sob, she pleaded, 'Oh, don't do this to me, Arden. Please don't. Not now, not when I'm...'

Shoving the door fully open, he dragged her into his arms, guided her towards the bed and sat with her on the edge. 'No more games, Rowan,' he said gently as he held her against him. 'I'm too old, too tired; even my brain aches.'

Swiftly contrite, she asked, 'Was it very bad?'

'Yes,' he said with a shudder. 'It was damned awful—and I really don't think I could be a fireman. I really don't think I could do that ever again. I ran in without thought. Stupid. And how I got up those burning stairs I will never know. I couldn't *see*, couldn't *breathe*.

'She'd told me the baby was in the back room and I thought, Easy; up the stairs, along the landing, last door on the left. Only when you can't see distances get distorted; you're disorientated, don't know where the hell you are. It was sheer luck that got me there, and stupidity that nearly killed us both.

'The baby's door was shut, which was fortunate because it had kept most of the smoke out. It was bad in there, but not disastrous—and I left the door open... I didn't even think! I mean, what's the first

rule of fires? Close the doors! So what did I do? Left
it open. I'd groped across to the cot, grabbed up baby,
bedding and all—and it was like a fireball hurtling
through the open door.

'Lord, Rowan—' he shuddered in remembered
horror '—that's when I thought I was going to die.
That's when I *knew* I was going to die, and if the
window had been made up of small panes, like at the
front, I *would* have died. If there had been safety bars,
no way would I have got out. And it must be true that
God looks after fools and drunks, because that window
was a wide glass square, the sort that pushes open from
the bottom, and I just tucked in my head, held the
baby tight, lowered my shoulder and charged.'

She found that she was grasping his hand very
tightly, found that she could see it all in horrifying
detail, and her long shudder matched his.

Blinking to clear his vision, he squeezed her hand,
then released it. 'Go and have your bath,' he instructed
her gently, 'before we both fall asleep as we are.'

With a tired nod, she went to run it.

Whilst she soaked away her aches and pains, held a
dampened cotton-wool pad to the cut over her eye,
she thought back over that long, long day and shook
her head in disbelief. When the door opened, she lazily
turned her head, and tiredly watched as Arden,
sweater now removed, walked in. He gave her an odd
smile, walked to the mirror over the washbasin and
stood regarding his dirty face. With a half-laugh, he
leaned his forearms along the rim of the basin and
stared down into the white porcelain.

'I'm getting too old for all this,' he muttered. 'I want
a bit of peace, Rowan. A bit of warmth in my life.

Love. And I'm so damned tired I could go to sleep where I stand.'

Her lovely eyes full of compassion and love and despair, she climbed slowly out, examined the pad of cotton wool, then tossed it into the bin. After emptying the water, she refilled the bath, and, wrapping herself in a towel, went to stand behind him. Briefly resting her cheek against his bowed back, savouring these last moments, she gave him the tiniest of hugs. 'Come on; let's wash this smoke and soot out of your hair. . . No, no, stay as you are.'

Reaching round him, she turned on the hot tap and let it run until the water was warm. Putting in the plug, she soaped her hands and began to wash his thick hair. Using the tooth mug, she rinsed it as best she could, wiped his dirty face, instructed him to wash his hands, then half pushed, half encouraged him towards the bath.

The removal of the rest of his clothing was a joint effort, and when he was hunched over in the bath she knelt down and soaped his back, then pushed him gently down into the water in order to reach his front. There were two nasty red patches on his chest which she supposed ought to have some cream on them, but, seeing as she didn't have any burn cream, she didn't mention the matter.

He lay back with his eyes closed and she stared at his strong face for a moment, remembered her fear, her anguish, remembered the good times. A bleak light in her beautiful eyes, she rinsed off his chest, shuffled along on her knees to soap his feet.

'OK, my brave warrior,' she murmured huskily, 'out you come.'

Without opening his eyes he gave a little grunt of acknowledgement, which meant that he'd heard her but probably wouldn't do anything about it. With a faint smile, she picked up his hand and tugged. 'Come on—bed.'

Opening his eyes, he gave a half-hearted grin. 'I'm going to hate myself for this in the morning. Two naked bodies, a nice warm bath. . .'

Only a joke, Rowan, she told herself sadly. Only a joke.

With a sigh, he levered himself upright, took the towel she offered him, hooked out the plug and climbed out. As his left foot touched the floor he winced. He would definitely have that X-rayed in the morning, she decided—and then remembered that she probably wouldn't be there. Even if he wanted her she couldn't spend the rest of her life watching what she said or didn't say, waiting for him to misunderstand.

And when she remembered his coldness she felt heartsick, because it was the same sort of coldness that her father used to display to punish her. And she really thought, all things considered, that she'd been punished enough. By everybody.

Walking before him into the bedroom, she held back the covers, waited until he'd climbed into bed—because to insist that he went home would have been cruel—then tucked him warmly up.

'Close your eyes,' she said softly.

He grunted, turned over and fell instantly asleep.

CHAPTER NINE

ROWAN debated sleeping in the armchair, lying on top of the covers, but she wanted to hold him, needed to hold him, because she loved him. Had always loved him—never, perhaps, more so than now—and if Patricia was going to have him for the rest of his life. . . Would she begrudge her just this one night? Of course she would.

Too tired even to think straight, Rowan climbed in beside him, snuggled against his warm body and thankfully lowered weighted lids. She stirred briefly when she heard the fire engines finally arrive but was too tired to do more than register the fact.

It was gone ten the next morning when they finally woke within seconds of each other. They were curled warmly together, faces almost touching, arms round each other, legs entwined. Lifting her lashes, Rowan stared into humorous grey eyes.

'This is nice,' he murmured.

'Yes,' she agreed sadly.

'This is *very* nice.'

'Yes.'

'And we've hurt each other enough, haven't we? Twelve months of stupidity is enough for anyone.'

'Yes,' she agreed.

'Twelve months of wanting, needing. . .'

Peace. 'Yes,' she repeated quickly before he could

complete the sentence. Before he could wish her well.
Invite her to his and Patricia's engagement party.

'I'd better get up.'

His face suddenly sober, he demanded, 'What's
wrong? Last night you—'

'Nothing.'

'Rowan,' he insisted quietly, 'what's wrong?'

Swallowing the hard lump in her throat, she whispered, 'Patricia. . .'

'Patricia?' He frowned. 'What about her?'

'She'll be waiting for you.'

'Will she? Why?'

'She was here. . .'

'She came in with Tom to see if they could help.
They could see the fire from the house. And Tom has
some news for me.'

'Oh. I. . .'

'Don't go,' he said softly, persuasively. 'We didn't
finish our talk. And perhaps this is the best way to do
it—naked and defenceless, all barriers down.'

'Oh, Arden. . .'

'Come on; we can't spend the rest of our lives—
wondering.'

With a sad little sigh, putting a bit more distance
between them because she couldn't bear the feel of
him, the touch, because she thought it would destroy
her, she watched him warily.

'It's been difficult this week, hasn't it?'

'An understatement,' she agreed with a funny little
smile.

'Yes. I did not want you here,' he said simply. 'I
determined to be cool, aloof, but you scramble under
my guard, Rowan. You always did. And seeing you

every day, seeing your smile, your frown, knowing you were in the same house, wanting to touch you, wanting to hurt you, has been purgatory. I wished I'd never met you—and I wished I'd never let you go.'

Staring at him, watching the changing expressions on that strong face, she decided that perhaps he was right. No matter how painful it might be, perhaps now was finally the time to be honest. 'I did love you, Arden.'

'Did you? Then why wouldn't you come back with me? Why so—adamant?'

'Because I was frightened,' she said simply, sadly. 'Because you pushed me into saying something I didn't altogether mean. I was angry. You were angry, and pride, or stupidity, wouldn't let me back down. I'd backed down so many times in my life, you see. And I don't think I really thought that it would end there. Not like that. But you didn't come back,' she sighed.

'But I did. Twice. And the first time you were draped round ape-man, the second round someone else.'

'And you couldn't *ask*?' she demanded sadly. 'Couldn't you even have *asked*?'

'No,' he said ruefully, 'because I couldn't envisage a future. And I wasn't going to beg.'

'I rang you,' she confessed quietly. 'But you were never there.'

'And you never left a message, did you?'

'No.'

'Why?'

'I don't know. Afraid you would come to fetch me, I suppose. And afraid that you wouldn't.'

'Wouldn't?' he asked with a frown.

'Mmm. If you didn't know I'd rung, you wouldn't come, but if you did know and didn't. . .'

'That's crazy.'

'No, it isn't. I couldn't have borne it, you see, if you hadn't come.'

'But I didn't. . .'

'No, because I didn't leave a message.'

'That's illogical.'

'Not to me, it isn't.'

'Good God, no wonder men never understand women.'

With a faint smile, she asked softly, 'Would you have come?'

'It would have depended,' he said carefully, 'on whether you'd changed your mind about coming to the States. I wasn't a toy to be picked up and cuddled when you had time.'

'You said that before,' she said softly.

'Yes. It was how I felt—ignored when you were busy, expected to fly over when you weren't. Would that really have satisfied you, Rowan? Not seeing each other for months at a time?'

'I thought it was an—option. Then,' she tacked on softly. 'Because I didn't know how it would feel to be without you. I'd had no experience of such a powerful emotion, had thought—stupidly—that it might work.'

'It would never have worked. Not for me. I wanted you with me all the time. Wanted you when the sun went down and when it rose in the morning. I loved you.'

'It didn't seem like it sometimes. Not towards the end, anyway.'

'Because you wouldn't bend, because if you'd loved

me you would have come back with me, adapted your plan—and because you knew that I couldn't adapt mine. And you told me not to come back. That you didn't want to see me again.'

'Because I thought you were punishing me.'

'Punishing you?' He frowned again.

'Yes. For daring to dream. The way my parents used to punish me. And I missed you so much that it was tearing me apart. I missed the security you gave me, the warmth, the love—only I couldn't admit that, could I? Because I was independent. Mistress of my own fate. I had a *plan*. And told everyone I had a plan. And so, when you did not, as I'd thought you would, come back, I made the plan bigger.'

'Became tougher, stronger and even more determined.'

'Yes,' she agreed sadly. 'The pretence had become reality. More or less, anyway. I put you away in my mind, pretended you didn't exist, pretended I did not need you, did not need anyone—and when I came to see Hetty I instructed myself very firmly on how I would behave. Cool, casual—calm,' she added even more wryly, 'because I *knew* that emotion was a killer of dreams.'

'And if I'd handled it differently? Handled you differently? Would you have come with me?'

'Knowing what I know now? Maybe. I don't know. I truly do not know,' she sighed. 'I hadn't known that feelings could be so intense. Hadn't really trusted them. I wanted it all—and didn't know how to choose. Small problems became large. Disagreements were magnified out of proportion, and those last few days, when I made a determined effort to talk to you, explain, you had no time.'

'Time,' he muttered with a sigh. 'The enemy of lovers. I had an auction I needed to go to, A Regency desk I so desperately wanted for a client, and I was hellishly late... A year of bitterness because of a desk,' he murmured.

'And instead of telling me why, explaining, you just said crossly that you had no time for immature tantrums.'

'Did I?'

'Yes.'

He gave a comical grimace. 'Not very tactful.'

'No.'

'Nor lover-like.'

'No. You treated me like an empty-headed fool, as though my concerns just didn't *matter*. And they did, Arden; they did. I'd spent my whole life fighting to be someone. Fighting to be taken seriously... And it *hurt* that my plans were dismissed as foolish.'

'I never said they were foolish—just damned inconvenient.'

'But you wouldn't *discuss* them, let me explain! Why?' she demanded in remembered puzzlement. 'Why could you not at least listen?'

'Because... I don't know,' he confessed. 'Because...'

'Because you thought I was being arbitrary, because you thought I should immediately fall in with your own plans—because mine were only fledgling,' she added softly. 'You refused to see me as a woman with a brain, a need, an ability.'

'No! My God, Rowan, you make it sound as though I thought you were some sort of bimbo!'

'No, not a bimbo, just someone—decorative,' she said bitterly. 'Do you have any idea how much I hate being decorative?'

He grunted with amusement. 'A lot of people wouldn't agree with you.'

'I know.'

'And I thought you were biting off more than you could chew... No, I wanted you with me and couldn't, or wouldn't, understand why, if you *must* run a business, you couldn't run it over here! I had the connections, could have helped...'

'I didn't want you to help! You still don't understand, do you? I had to do it! By myself! It had to be *me* in charge. Me who thought of it, me who fought, me who executed it! Me! You would have taken over,' she continued more quietly, 'improvised, improved— and it wouldn't have been mine. And you'd probably have done it better, more efficiently, and—oh, Arden, I couldn't have borne that. I couldn't.'

'Then why on earth didn't you say?'

'I *tried*. But we never talked, did we?' she said sadly. 'Never really sat down and talked, discussed things. You just wanted...'

'To love you,' he said simply.

'But it didn't *feel* like that! It felt like being caged! My parents caged me, hedged me about with restrictions. If I'd been amiable, easygoing, instead of competitive, determined, maybe there wouldn't now be this alienation from them, but I am like that, and eventually, after years of being goody two shoes, of never getting dirty, never playing with unsuitable

people, having friends chosen for me, *lessons* chosen
for me, I rebelled. And when I transgressed, kicked
against the restrictions, I was treated to silence—
disapproval without words.

'I was pretty and delicate and special,' she said
bitterly. 'Treated like a doll, dressed up, paraded,
shown off! But I wasn't allowed to be *me*! A prize
heifer!

'I could come top of the class because that was
something that could be boasted about, but I couldn't
go to university because that meant I would pick up
unsuitable ideas, mix with the wrong people, live away
from home—and that wasn't to be thought of.

'There would be drugs, marches, protests, and supposing I got caught up in all that? No, no, Rowan had
to stay home with Mummy and Daddy. But I didn't
want to stay home getting older and duller and more
and more frustrated. I wanted to spread my wings!
And I feel so *guilty*!' she cried.

'Dear God,' he said softly, 'how long has all that
been bottled up?'

'For ever!' She shuddered. 'Oh, Arden,' she sighed.
'I was the prettiest, the brightest, the best dressed, the
most *hated* girl in my school. The other kids mocked
the way I spoke, the way I was forced to dress. . . I was
teacher's pet, Daddy's darling. . . My parents even took
me to school, collected me. . . At five it was acceptable,
but at *sixteen*? I was stifled and hurting. . . I hated it,
Arden. Came to hate it so much, and they couldn't see
why. Still don't see why.'

'And then I came along and *I* tried to clip those
newly fledged wings.'

'Yes. And as the weeks went by without you I told

myself I didn't need you, that the—affair had been a mistake—a mistake that must be buried, and if you tell yourself something often enough in the end you begin to believe it. Yet when I walked into your office a whole year later I knew I hadn't buried it deep enough.'

'And I sneered, didn't I?'

'Yes.'

Holding her eyes with his own, he said softly, earnestly, 'I'm not sneering now.'

'No.' But now it was too late.

'And a close shave with death is a wonderful way of focusing the mind. Makes you realise how stupid it is to waste time. Makes you realise how petty everything else is.'

'Yes.' And because, even now, she needed to know, she asked, 'Were there other women?'

'No.'

Patricia? she wondered as she continued to stare into his eyes.

'Oh, I met plenty; wealthy men do,' he said with a trace of cynicism. 'But they weren't you. Didn't have your glorious temper. Didn't have your warmth, your courage, your laughter. Didn't beat me up, didn't have your capacity for passion. Didn't have anything at all that I wanted. None of them could hold a candle to my glorious Rowan. My compulsion. You were wilful, arrogant, beautiful, sensuous and appealing, and I wanted you. I have never wanted anyone as I wanted you.

'I didn't think I would marry, didn't even expect to fall in love. I'd reached the age of thirty-four without doing so, and then Hetty asked me to deliver some things to you. . .and everything changed.

'I couldn't stop thinking about you, couldn't stop wanting to touch you, hold you. You filled my dreams, my waking thoughts, and I wanted you. A little bit crazy, perhaps, but I'd never felt like that, and I didn't want the madness to end. You were an obsession almost, and part of me resented it—this power you had over me; and so when you refused to come to the States, threw everything back in my face, the resentment turned to hate.'

'But not indifference?' she asked softly.

'No, Rowan, not indifference. And you? What of those men who dragged you to the edge of passion?' he mocked gently. 'How many of them were there?'

With one of her funny little smiles, she admitted, 'None.'

'None?' He smiled. 'Not one?'

'No, not one—and there's no need to sound so smug, because there might have been.'

'You think I don't know that? Think I'm not aware that you're every man's fantasy?'

'Every man's what?' she asked in embarrassed astonishment. 'Don't be daft.'

'Not daft. Men *want* you, Rowan. You're vibrant, alive, gloriously—exotic! Different. You have the most delightfully wicked smile, so warm and special, and I can't believe that no man—'

'I didn't say that no man had propositioned me! I said I hadn't. . . Not that I wouldn't have done,' she muttered defiantly, 'Because I would! When you didn't come back, when I finally decided you weren't going to, were *never* going to, I would have slept with every damned man I came across! Every single blessed one!'

'Then why didn't you?' he asked with a humorous little quirk to his mouth.

Lowering her lashes, she admitted honestly, 'Because they weren't you. Because none of them ever made me feel the way you could make me feel. They were either wimps or arrogant or petty or—there was just never any spark. Anyway, I didn't want another lover, not one that could make me *feel*. Emotion—hurts.'

'Yes, it does,' he agreed quietly. 'And if you'd told me all this then, about your parents—' Breaking off, he sighed.

'You would have what?' she queried gently.

'I don't know,' he admitted ruefully.

'No. Anyway, I never tell anyone what they're like, because—well, because it always smacks of disloyalty—and because everyone thinks I'm lucky to have such a nice, caring family. Adults do, anyway. And I feel continually guilty that I can't be the person they want me to be.'

'And did you view me as another adult?'

'Perhaps. You *were* older. . .'

'Not *that* much!'

'But certainly more experienced than me.'

'Yes, and perhaps I did want you caged,' he admitted, 'and couldn't, or wouldn't, understand your need for freedom. You were too damned attractive for your own good. Or mine. I didn't want other men to look at you, admire you, want you.'

'And anyone who did you automatically assumed I was having an affair with.'

'No,' he denied, 'not when we were together. I don't suffer from insecurity,' he said drily.

'Just a burning need to be right. Arrogant.'

'All my family are arrogant. My father was, my mother, and Hetty certainly is. Or perhaps it wasn't arrogance,' he qualified softly. 'Perhaps it was fear. Fear of losing you. Fear of giving you too much leeway in case you proved me wrong.

'I knew, logically, that I should have let you have your head, let you get it out of your system, but I wanted you, Rowan. I had *never* wanted anyone like I wanted you. And I wanted you *then*, not a year later—and because of that I brought about the very thing I was trying to prevent. And when I saw what a success you'd made of your life without me, saw you with those men, I told myself I was better off without you—which was self-deception at its worst.

'And when you finally arrived in Boston and, like you, I found that the pain was still there, the violent attraction was still there, I tried to close my mind to it, but I was having a foul week—and you prodded my temper, managed to say just the wrong thing at just the wrong time. . .'

'Because of the dirty-tricks campaign?'

'Yes. Damaging rumours that I'm going bankrupt, can't pay debts, that my antiques aren't genuine, my tourist boats are unseaworthy. . .'

'You run trips to see the whales, don't you?'

'Mmm, further north.'

'And, of course, people believe these rumours.'

'*Some* people.'

'You know who it is?'

'Oh, yes.'

'But have no proo— Ah. Is that what Tom was talking about? That he thinks there's now proof? He used to be a lawyer, didn't he?'

'Yes.'

'And this man is going to pay, isn't he?' she asked softly.

'Oh, yes, Rowan,' he said grimly. 'He is certainly going to pay.'

'In his own coin?'

'No. I'll take him to court.'

She could almost pity this unknown rival. Almost. It was a brave man or woman who would take on Arden and expect to win. Yet she'd expected to win, hadn't she? Searching his eyes, searching out her own truth, perhaps, she commented quietly, 'I did need to grow, Arden, needed to prove something to myself, needed the confidence those months brought me. And if we'd met now for the first time. . .'

'The beginning would have been the same—but, hopefully, not the ending we managed then.' With a gentle hand, he reached out to smooth back her tangled hair. 'Would it?'

She shook her head without looking at him. 'I didn't understand that loving someone changed the rules so dramatically. Didn't understand that I cared too much.'

'Can one care too much?'

'I think so. Loving needs to be tempered with wisdom, understanding, and good relationships aren't something that either of us cut our eye-teeth on. Your own parents were pretty arbitrary, weren't they?'

'Arbitrary? No.' He smiled. 'Just hung up on the American dream—be a winner, achieve great things.'

'As you did.'

'Yes.'

'Hetty had a lover; did you know?' she asked idly.

'Mmm? Oh, yes. And why have we changed the subject?'

'He died.'

His smile was wry.

'That's why she wanted us back together. Said chances don't come twice.'

'Don't they?' he asked gently. 'I loved you, Rowan, wanted you, and stupidly thought that should be enough.'

'Thought I should be grateful?' she asked with a smile.

'No, but understanding, perhaps. Fighting to be an achiever, maybe I grew too hard, too arrogant, too determined, and didn't, or wouldn't, understand your frustration, your needs. . .'

'Any more than I understood yours. And yet we of all people should have understood each other. We both wanted to make our own mark on the world, not extend someone else's—me with my father, you with yours.'

'Mmm. I rowed with him a lot too,' he added whimsically.

'You row with everyone.'

He laughed, then sobered. 'Would you really have come back if I'd crooked my little finger?'

'After my club took off? I don't know. If we'd talked the way we're talking now, if I could have retained part of my independence. Would you?'

'Yes.'

'Without qualification?'

'Ah.' With a wry grin, he admitted, 'Possibly not.

But the question never arose, did it? Because we were both too afraid of losing our identity. I'm unbelievably proud of you, though—of your success.'

'Arden,' she protested, 'don't tell fibs.'

'I'm not.' He smiled. 'Wild horses wouldn't have dragged the admission out of me prior to this, but I am. It took a lot of guts to do what you did—a lot of determination.'

'No,' she said softly, 'it was built on desperation, fear of failure.' And then, taking her courage in both hands, she asked bluntly, 'Did our lovemaking yesterday really mean nothing to you?'

'I didn't say it didn't mean anything,' he replied gently. 'I don't think I said anything. At first, after it happened, I was confused, not sure what I wanted, not sure how you felt—afraid of making a fool of myself, I suppose, not sure I could go through it all again. And then I stood in the study with Patricia, not listening to one blessed word she said because all I could think about was you, all I could see was the pain in your lovely eyes... And so I walked out on her mid-flow— and found you'd gone. All packed up and gone. You couldn't have gone *far*—I hadn't heard the phone so you couldn't have called for a cab—therefore the only logical thing for you to have done was walk to the village. And only you would do so in a force-nine gale!'

'I was desperate,' she said, miffed.

'Were you?'

'Yes.'

'I was worried.'

'You thought I might meet a moose?'

He gave her a look of reproof. 'You're afraid of the dark, aren't you?'

'No,' she denied with an aloof little toss of her head. 'I just don't like it very much.'

With a wry smile at her qualification, he continued, 'So I grabbed my car keys and hurried after you. I'd easily catch you on the road, I told myself. . . What did you do? Run?'

'No.'

'And then, suddenly, there you were. Perfectly safe, perfectly in command, or so I thought, and busily coping. And that hurt me more, I found.'

'Hurt?' she queried carefully.

'Yes. I wanted you to rely on me, I suppose. Needed that. I'd been—frightened, afraid, sure of your hurt and bewilderment; I'd rushed around to rescue you from your fear of the dark, and you seemed to be suffering nothing of the sort.' Smiling at her, seeming not to notice her stillness, he added humorously, 'I really do think, Rowan, that in order for this to work we have to learn to talk. Like really *talk*!'

'For what to work?'

'What?' he asked comically.

'For what to work?' she repeated.

His face changing, a frown etched on his forehead, he said quietly, 'for us to get back together. Dear God, Rowan, don't do this to me!'

Frozen, almost forgetting to breathe, she whispered, 'And what about Patricia?'

'Patricia? What about Patricia?'

'You're going to marry her. . .'

'Don't be absurd! I *never* had any intention of marrying Patricia! She knows it and I know it.'

'She called you darling. . .'

'She calls everyone darling.'

'You kissed her.'

'*She* kissed me!' he exclaimed in exasperation.

'Why?'

'Because I'd agreed to let her landscape the wretched garden! Because I wasn't in the mood, because I wasn't thinking. I'd walked out in a temper, in confusion, needed to think, and she caught me up, babbled on about trellises and summer houses—didn't I think this, didn't I think that, and please, please would I let her do it? To get rid of her, I agreed! She followed me into the study, shoved plans under my nose. . .'

'But you allowed me to think. . .'

'Of course I did! I didn't think you wanted me back.'

'How do you know I do now?' she asked tartly.

'Don't you?'

'Yes!' she exclaimed brokenly. Hurling herself into his arms, she held him impossibly tight. 'Why didn't you say?' she demanded, her voice muffled in his warm shoulder.

'Oh, Rowan,' he murmured as the hug was fiercely returned. 'Because I thought you were being cautious! Because you were still unsure of your feelings!'

'I've never been unsure of my feelings, you idiot!'

'Charming.' With a snort of laughter, he eased her slightly away, grinned into her lovely face. 'That's what I mean about talking!'

'Mmm.' With a delightfully roguish smile, her thighs finally, beautifully touching his, she ran her tongue along his collar-bone, savoured the taste of him, the scent. 'Perhaps we should tack a notice over the bed to that effect,' she mused huskily.

'At the foot of the bed,' he argued, equally husky, 'so that we can see it at all times.'

'At all times?' she queried softly, and her eyes were darker, her voice thicker.

'Most of the time,' he corrected himself throatily. 'Sometimes you will, of course, be tied to the kitchen sink.'

'Mmm.' Lowering her lashes, which would have made anyone else look coy but which made Rowan look nothing of the sort, she murmured, 'You're—um—aroused.'

'So are you.'

'Mmm. And although I'm not sure I should forgive you for your brutality on the landing...'

'I was fighting a rearguard action.'

'I think it's also best to tell you that I'm not—er—taking precautions. Which means...'

'If we do what we are most definitely intending to do, we could be into nappies before the year is out.' His own eyes dark, almost black, as they held hers, one warm palm touching, stroking her, he added, 'Although that's a bit like bolting the stable door... And I'm not getting any younger,' he murmured provocatively.

'No. Neither am I.'

With a smile that was meant to be sly and looked only shaken, he urged her closer, dragged in a sharp breath as he gave in to the spark they had both been trying to ignore whilst they'd talked. And as their mouths met their bodies automatically flowed together, Arden above, Rowan below, his legs straight, hers bent, knees raised, clasping his thighs.

The warmth of him, the feel of him made her shiver, hold him tighter. There were words of endearment, passion, need, brief laughter as he murmured thickly, 'I liked it better with suspender belt and stockings.'

And then his tongue was touching hers, pressing, mouths were open, bodies clasped impossibly tight, until with a groan he slid his hands beneath her buttocks, raised her slightly, found the warmth he needed, as did she.

She raised her feet, crossed her ankles tight against his powerful thighs, gave little cries of pleasure, thrust fiercely against him, loved him with every part of her, held nothing back, dug her fingers into his spine until he arched closer, until the rhythm was perfect, until it felt as though they would fuse into one being—until his release freed them both.

'Oh, Rowan,' he mumbled into her warm neck. 'Rowan, Rowan, Rowan. How I have needed that. How I have needed you.'

She stared past his tousled hair, stared upwards, trailed her fingers lovingly up and down his strong back—a soothing, erotic passage—then clutched him tightly as she silently vowed that if biting her tongue on occasion was what it took to put his needs before her own then that was what she would do, because never, *ever* would she relinquish this again. Never would she give the opportunity to some other woman—someone like Patricia, perhaps. He was hers. He had always been hers—as she had always been his.

'I love you,' she said desperately. 'I have always loved you. And, oh, Arden, I need so very badly to be loved back. Loved as *me*. Not how I should be, how I could be, but as *me*.'

Raising his head, he gazed down into her exquisite face. 'You are loved back. You will always be loved back. I swear. I don't think you have *any* idea how much I missed you.'

Moving her hands, touching her fingers to his face as though she were blind and needed to read him, rubbing her knuckles across his stubbled jaw, she whispered, 'I know what it was like trying to live without you—hard sometimes, desperately hard. But I did not know how it could ever work between us. And then you were so hurtful, said it was too late, and I gave up, or tried to tell myself I had—until I thought you had died inside.

'And, Arden, nothing—*nothing*,' she emphasised, 'will ever frighten me as much again. When I thought you were dead—No,' she corrected herself, 'when I *knew* you were dead, I suddenly realised that there was no point to anything, that without you the effort of living would be just too great. Why did I never admit that before? Why did I never see my stupid, stubborn pride for what it was?'

'Perhaps because all your formative years were filled with rejection, manipulation, and you were just too damned scared to put it to the test.'

'Perhaps, but *you've* never been scared.'

'Not of physical challenges, no. Nor even mental ones. But emotion, Rowan? Emotion scared the hell out of me. Emotion made you weak, vulnerable....'

'Is that why you always pretended to be hard?'

'Perhaps.' With a funny little grimace, he planted a kiss in the centre of her forehead. 'God only knows what I'll be like if we have children. I'll be a nervous wreck. I'll be afraid to let them out of my sight.'

'Build them cages?' she asked softly, a little sadly.

'Yes. But without the bars. I promise.' Then, with a quirky grin, he added, 'Although, knowing you, if I did ever make the mistake of leaving bars, my lovely Rowan would bash them down, wouldn't she?'

'She would,' she confirmed. 'We'll work it out,' she added reassuringly. 'We *have* to.'

'Yes,' he agreed sombrely, 'we do.'

'And I'm not nearly so fiery as I was,' she assured him. 'I'm much more controlled. Adult.'

'You are?' he asked in tones of severe disappointment. 'Oh, well, in that case I'm not sure that I want you back. Ouch,' he added as she hit him. 'I'm *wounded*, Rowan!' he reproached her.

'Not that wounded,' she scoffed lightly. 'Didn't affect your performance any, did it?'

'No-o,' he agreed thoughtfully, 'although it wasn't that bit of me that was wounded.'

Laughing, she released herself and rolled free. 'Do you realise what the time is? Midday! And I'm *starving*!' Padding into the bathroom, her mouth curved in a lovely smile, she cleaned her teeth, had a wash, then padded back into the bedroom. Arden was sitting on the edge of the bed examining his wounds, and her smile died as she saw the angry red patches on his hands and chest. 'Hospital for you, my lad,' she said softly.

Looking up as though surprised to see her back, he grinned, and it was the Arden of long ago—the wonderful, loving, teasing Arden, the man she had loved so passionately, the handsome stranger, the hero who

would slay all her dragons. 'I love you!' she exclaimed
fervently.

With a blink of surprise, he caught her hands and
pulled her between his thighs. 'I know you do. Don't
look so—anguished, darling. It will be all right. I'll
make it all right.'

'Then don't run into any more burning buildings,
will you?'

'No.' Dragging her closer, he pressed a kiss to her
tummy, then slapped her lightly on her bottom. '*You*
have clean clothes to wear. *I* will have to go around
looking like a burned tramp.'

'Want me to pop back to the house to get you some
clean clothes?'

Shaking his head, he said, 'We'll call in on our way
to the hospital.'

'To get your ankle X-rayed?'

'To check on the baby—and see if Hetty is ready to
be released,' he added slowly as memory of his aunt
returned. 'Oh, hell, I'd forgotten all about Hetty
coming home today.'

'Then whilst I find out if she's ready you can get
your foot X-rayed, can't you?' she said firmly. Glancing
down, she dropped into a squat to feel his ankle gently.
'It's a bit puffy.'

'It's also damned sore, and I just *love* this wifely
concern. I think you should always kneel before me; I
think it should be written into the marriage contract.'

'So do I.' She grinned. 'Especially when the lord and
master has no clothes on.' Scampering out of his reach,
she picked up her bag and began to remove clean
clothing whilst he went into the bathroom—then hur-

riedly followed and gave him a fierce hug. 'Isn't this *nice*?' she exclaimed happily.

Turning, surprised once again, he laughed. 'Yes. It is.'

Satisfied, she walked back into the bedroom, and heard him give a rich chuckle. Echoing it, she began to dress, and when they were both ready and had exchanged a lingering, loving kiss he opened the door—and burst out laughing.

Going to see what had so amused him, she grinned. Someone had hung a 'Do not disturb' sign on the door.

'Tactful,' he murmured.

'Very.' She took his hand, and together they went downstairs to discover if Betty could feed them.

Driving towards the hospital, out of the blue, or as though the subject had continued to bother him, Arden asked almost casually, 'And you were never—intimate with your manager?'

'Donald? Good grief, no. He's happily married.'

With a sideways glance, he commented softly, 'Then I bet he made sure his wife never caught sight of you.'

Startled, she grinned, then burst out laughing.

'Well, did she?'

'No.'

'Wise man. What will you do about the gym?' he added quietly.

Taking the plunge, and before she could change her mind, she said firmly, 'Give it up.'

'What?'

'Watch where you're going!' she ordered in alarm as the car beiefly swerved.

'Sorry.' Pulling over, he switched off the engine.
'What did you say?'

'That I would give it up.'

'But you love it!'

'Now, you aren't trying to persuade me to *keep* it,
are you?' she teased.

'No, but. . .'

'It would make you feel guilty?' she queried softly.
'Good.' Then she grinned. 'But we do have to talk
about it, don't we? And I do like it here. I didn't think
I would, you know, but I do.'

He wisely kept silent.

With a thoughtful frown, she began again, 'For some
time now I seem to have been getting further and
further away from what I love doing, what I originally
intended to do. From being a straightforward stress
centre with aromatherapy, reflexology and the sale of
aromatic oils, suddenly we were into fitness cycles,
gymnasium equipment, designs for a pool. People
asked for this or that—did we have a sauna, a sun
room?—and because it was a challenge to provide
what they wanted, a need to prove myself, I suppose,
like Topsy, it began to grow.

'And now there's more administration than actual
hands-on working, because without quite realising
what I was doing I began delegating more and more of
the actual therapy sessions to my staff. Oh, it was
exciting and rewarding, but I began to miss the client
contact, only, of course by that time I had employed
enough therapists to cope with the load and done
myself out of what I liked doing best.'

'Sadly that's true of most owner-run businesses.'

'Yes. So what I need is a change.'

'To do what?'

Still the same old arrogant Arden, she thought with a little grin. He'd get a bit of a shock if she told him that she wanted to build a fitness centre in Hong Kong.

'And why the smile?' he asked softly. 'Because you think I automatically assume you'll want to do something near here? Not so—' Breaking off, he gave a wry grin. 'Is so. Well, go on,' he said fatalistically. 'You want to go to Tibet, right?'

'No,' she laughed, 'Hong Kong. No, I don't. What I would really like, I think, is to allow Donald to manage the fitness centre and just pop over once or twice a year, or even let him buy me out or something. But I do need a measure of independence, even if it's only to earn pocket money. I need. . .'

'The comfort of a safety net in case it all goes wrong?'

'No, not that—never that—but to feel that if I need anything, want anything—something silly, something small, just a pair of stockings—I won't have to *ask*.'

'I know what you're saying, Rowan, but don't you think I might have a need to provide for you? Lavish gifts on you? A need to spoil? I have no one to spoil. Hetty doesn't need anything. . .'

'Stop trying to sound pathetic. And you can spoil me all you like.' She grinned.

'Thank you,' he said drily. 'I'm not trying to say you can't have a business. . .'

'Good. Don't rush me, Arden,' she begged softly. 'I can't let go all at once. I'll maybe come round to that when it's more familiar, when I'm. . .'

'Sure?'

'No. I *am* sure—sure that I can't live without you,

but I'm not sure I would be very comfortable living *off* you.'

'Oh, Rowan.'

'No, don't scoff; try to understand, please. My parents never wanted me to work; they needed the control of providing for me, governing my actions. Do you know how humiliating it is having to ask for everything you need? Account for every penny you spend?'

'Rowan,' he chided gently, 'I do understand, and as long as you're on the same side of the Atlantic, as long as you're *with* me. . .'

She smiled. 'Sorry. But what I would like is to open a small salon where I can get back to—basics, if you like. I miss the little chats with clients, the challenge, the personal satisfaction gained from making people feel better, calmer.'

'Yes, I can understand that. So?' he asked a trifle cautiously.

'So, do you think Maine, or Boston, or wherever it is we are going to live, is ready for a fully qualified, really amiable aromatherapist?'

'Amiable?' he queried as he fought the relieved grin that was tugging at his mouth.

'Mmm-hmm. It will be all right, won't it?' she blurted out.

'Oh, darling.' Oblivious of the traffic that was passing, the curious stares, he pulled her into his arms, held her impossibly tight. 'Of course it will,' he reassured her huskily. 'We'll be the happiest couple in the whole wide world!'

'Yes?'

'Yes.' Moving back a fraction, he searched her face.

'What is it? You sound hesitant and it's not like you to be negative.'

'I know,' she sighed. 'I'm just a bit frightened, I think.'

'Of me?'

'No, of failing again, of having it all go wrong.'

'Why should it? Neither of us will make the mistakes we made last time, and now that we *know* what's at stake, now that we have the "talk" notice. . .'

A faint smile in her eyes, she rested her forehead against his. 'Yes,now that we have the "talk" notice everything will be fine, won't it?'

'I think so. I think we'll be the happiest, the most goddamned envied couple in the whole world.'

'Yeah?' Winding her arms round his neck, she nestled closer and smiled. Yeah. Probably the most volatile as well. But that made for interest, didn't it? Excitement. Oh, yes, it definitely made for excitement.

'And in the meantime, whilst we're waiting for our family to arrive,' he chuckled, 'there's a little shop that I think will be just ri—'

'Arden,' she warned softly, drawing away from him slightly, 'it's very kind of you to take an interest, but if I do it I have to do it by myself.'

'Right, but it's in a really good po—'

'Arden.'

'Right.' Ostentatiously pressing his lips together, his eyes alight with laughter, he fought to remain uninvolved, uninterested—and failed miserably. 'You'd really like it,' he tried to persuade her softly. 'Green and gold sign: "Rowan, The Really Amiable Aromatherapist".'

'And reflexologist,' she put in as she fought a smile of her own.

'Mmm. I know a really good shopfitter—'

'I'll smack you in a minute.'

'Yeah?' Laughing delightedly, he hauled her back into his arms. 'All right, I'll let you do it all by your own self.'

'Promise?'

'Mmm.'

'OK.'

'I love you.'

'Good.' Her smile widening, she nestled into him again. 'I might let you help a little bit.'

Fighting for solemnity, he sensibly kissed her before she could retaliate.

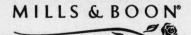

Anne Mather

Collection

This summer Mills & Boon brings you a powerful
collection of three passionate love stories from
an outstanding author of romance:

Tidewater Seduction
Rich as Sin
Snowfire

576 pages of passion, drama and
compelling story lines.

Available: August 1996

MILLS & BOON®

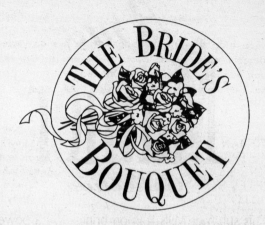

Three women make a pact to stay single,
but one by one they fall, seduced by the
power of love!

Don't miss Penny Jordan's exciting new
miniseries—The Brides Bouquet coming to
you in the new Mills & Boon Presents line
in September 1996.

Look out for:

Woman to Wed? in September
Best Man to Wed? in October
Too Wise to Wed? in January '97

MILLS & BOON®

Next Month's Romances

Each month you can choose from a wide variety of romance with Mills & Boon. Below are the new titles to look out for next month in our two new series Presents and Enchanted.

Presents™

WOMAN TO WED?	Penny Jordan
MISTRESS MATERIAL	Sharon Kendrick
FINN'S TWINS!	Anne McAllister
AFTER HOURS	Sandra Field
MR LOVERMAN	Mary Lyons
SEDUCED	Amanda Browning
THE FATHER OF HER CHILD	Emma Darcy
A GUILTY AFFAIR	Diana Hamilton

Enchanted™

A KISS FOR JULIE	Betty Neels
AN INNOCENT CHARADE	Patricia Wilson
THE RIGHT HUSBAND	Kay Gregory
THE COWBOY WANTS A WIFE!	Susan Fox
PART-TIME WIFE	Jessica Hart
BRIDES FOR BROTHERS	Debbie Macomber
GETTING OVER HARRY	Renee Roszel
THREE LITTLE MIRACLES	Rebecca Winters

One to Another

A year's supply of Mills & Boon® novels— absolutely FREE!

Would you like to win a year's supply of heartwarming and passionate romances? Well, you can and they're FREE! Simply complete the missing word competition below and send it to us by 28th February 1997. The first 5 correct entries picked after the closing date will win a year's supply of Mills & Boon romance novels (six books every month—worth over £150). What could be easier?

PAPER	B A C K	WARDS
ARM		MAN
PAIN		ON
SHOE		TOP
FIRE		MAT
WAIST		HANGER
BED		BOX
BACK		AGE
RAIN		FALL
CHOPPING		ROOM

Please turn over for details of how to enter 🖙

How to enter...

There are ten missing words in our grid overleaf.
Each of the missing words must connect up with the
words on either side to make a new word—e.g.
PAPER-BACK-WARDS. As you find each one, write it in
the space provided, we've done the first one for you!

When you have found all the words, don't forget to fill in
your name and address in the space provided below and
pop this page into an envelope (you don't even need a
stamp) and post it today. Hurry—competition ends
28th February 1997.

Mills & Boon® One to Another
FREEPOST
Croydon
Surrey
CR9 3WZ

Are you a Reader Service Subscriber?   Yes ❑   No ❑

Ms/Mrs/Miss/Mr _____

Address _____

_____

_____ Postcode _____

One application per household.

You may be mailed with other offers from other reputable companies as a
result of this application. If you would prefer not to receive such offers,
please tick box.   ❑

C496
A

mps
MAILING
PREFERENCE
SERVICE